Jesus

In

Prison

A Study and Pray experience.

Roy Catchpole

CONTENTS

FOREWORD

One of the tragedies of the modern social scene is the ever-increasing volume of crime. One of its ironies is that prison rarely improves the criminal. If he tries to 'go straight', few employers will give him a responsible job, and even fewer of his neighbours will forget that he is an 'ex-con'.

However, nobody is too bad for Jesus to accept. Roy's story is an example of this. Once a man welcomes Jesus into his life, things begin to happen. Jesus can change men's lives - that's why he came. Also - and this is why Christianity is scandalous - nobody's too good to need Jesus' acceptance. There's no first and second-class travel into the Kingdom of God.

When Jesus begins to change a person's life, the change is striking. He takes up residence inside a person's life and changes their heart, desires, and attitudes. That change may be slow but it will be sure. He helps people to go 'straight' – both good people and bad. Christ is making a new man of Roy. I know, because I have been very closely associated with him during the past four years. Christ can make new people of all of us. He accepts us just as we are, but does not leave us where we were.

"If any person is in Christ, a new creation has come into being. The old passes away. Look! Everything has become new." 1 Corinthians 5:17

Jesus not only changes us, and accepts us, but also employs us. As Christians we are saved to serve. Roy has been saved to serve in the ordained ministry of the Church of England. Like John

Newton, the criminal who became a clergyman, Roy Catchpole has begun to build up what he used to destroy, and this book is the first part of his story. It is written with tremendous pace; as fresh as tomorrow's newspaper and amusing, honest and perceptive into the bargain. It sketches a picture of the effect the penal system has on young offenders; gives an encouraging picture of Christ's power to set men free on a deeper level; and draws an exhilarating picture of earthy, realistic Christian living after the prison gates opened.

MICHAEL GREEN

Principal

St.John's Theological College,

Nottingham

Biographical Outline

Roy Catchpole trained at St.John's College, Nottingham in England and was ordained into the Anglican priesthood in 1974, working mainly in U.K., inner city parishes.

On gaining his Masters degree in Theology and Ministry, he resigned his parish in 1994, spending the following two years in a Franciscan friary, concentrating his energies on a radical self-assessment to discover the sources of his faith and to reappraise his life. A father to three, he is divorced and remarried.

His evangelical Christian faith was radically challenged by his pilgrimage with Jesus among the Franciscans, many of whom were gay priests. Since the first edition of 'Key To Freedom' in 1975, his understanding of Jesus has been transformed. As a way of investigating the implications of this for his faith, and for the future of his mother Communion, he is currently engaged in empirical theological research into Christian Ministry.

A newspaper columnist for ten years, he has contributed to Thought for the Day, News At Ten and a number of religious programmes. He is the author of two books on Christian discipleship, and a textbook on the Elements of Christianity. He has lectured on Ethics, New Testament Theology and Mythology at Southampton University's School of Cultural Studies (University College) in Winchester, and on World Religions for the Workers' Educational

Association, and on Contemporary Christianity for St.John's Theological College (Trent University), in Nottingham. He is a regular contributor to the Religious and Theological Academic Abstracts CD Rom.

Prayer Guide and Reading Plan

This is not an ordinary book. At the end of each chapter is a reflection on the first Easter and other verses in the Bible that talk about the death of Jesus. The death and resurrection of Jesus are the foundation of Roy's Christian faith. The death of Jesus demonstrates the extent of God's love for all people. Whether these verses are familiar or new to you, ask God to bring the words alive to you and help you to know His love for you in a deep way.

LOOKING BACK

As I look back through the lens of forty years I can still see the angst-ridden, skinny teenager looking out over the little city of Rochester, England. Having spent three years enclosed in institutions, though he was in his early twenties he was, I can now see, a vulnerable child.

It was a cold, miserable morning. Ignoring church spires, leaky gargoyles, the splash of rain on cobbles and the impatient clatter of hunched people with umbrellas in the anonymous city, he fearfully imagined what it would be like to walk among them, pretending that he, like them, was normal. Not really knowing what he had got himself into by becoming a Christian, he imagined no one would notice him. Life would be better. It was a shot in the dark, because for the past three years he had been penned-up in prison, isolated from the rest of the community.

How much had things really changed? Would he be like a creature from outer space among normal people?

Having been brought to the young offenders' institution in the back of a prison van many months before, he had only ever once seen anything of the city of Rochester.   This had been for his Christian Confirmation at age twenty.

Resulting from arguments and studies with a Cambridge Chaplain and two Franciscan Friars, he had become a Christian in April 1966, and was confirmed by the bishop in the cathedral two weeks ago. Much else had also changed in his world that he was unaware of however.

In the past three years, while he had been hidden behind prison walls, Labour had come back into power under the leadership of Harold Wilson. From 1966, homosexual acts between consenting adults were now no longer illegal, abortion was more readily accessible, and the Divorce Reform Act had made it easier to end marriages. Roy had no way of knowing how this would impact on his life, but despite Mary Whitehouse and Lord Longford's efforts to launch a power-base for a moral minority in British political and religious life, a new liberal age had begun during his time in custody. In terms of Christian faith this was to lead to the current crisis in the Anglican Communion between Conservative and Liberal Christianity. The outcome is still in the balance.

Later on, when looking for work after his prison term, with the bad relations between government and the unions, Roy was fortunate to get a secure job in which the cuts in public spending, that affected his parents who were dependent on welfare benefits, had little affect on his own poor standard of living.

It was morning, and a transparent, cold mist hung about on the hills. The air was sweet with the smell of crushed Kentish hops and fresh mown grass - deep green, wet and trodden-on. The little city in the distance twinkled because of the moisture on its roofs and pavements as the budding day, with his new life, began to open-up.

The wall, with its spiked double gates topped with curled razor wire was behind the skinny adolescent. It looked less forbidding from the exterior side – not so forbidding or threatening as it had been for the boy who had, a few moments ago, been its prisoner. One lad had pensioned off a prison officer with a brick smashed down on his head in a failed escape a few months earlier. The lad had been pinioned on the razor wire like a wild animal in a trap, and was left there for a long time before being brought down. They had said they lacked the manpower... It was before the days of Child Protection and lacked the resultant mercy of political correctness. The child wondered if in the future, Australians would visit this place out of inquisitiveness to see where, at one time, people had been executed or imprisoned prior to being deported to their new country. It had been throughout that time that people were hanged at Rochester. He had been taken on a grisly tour, by one of the guards, to the room where the gallows used to be. The actual apparatus of death had not been there of course, but he knew that all it needed was a right-wing majority and an Act of Parliament. Most ordinary British wanted it the death penalty, and there would be no shortage of applicants to pull the lever.

Many years later the prison was to undergo an inspection by Sir David Ramsbotham, Her Majesty's Chief Inspector of Prisons, in which he was saddened to have to report, after a brilliant female prison governor had departed the prison, that,

'Looking after young prisoners is a specialist occupation, in which good staff/prisoner relationships are crucial. The key factor in these is mutual trust, built up by the same staff dealing with the same young prisoners, day after day, fairly, firmly and consistently. Yet staff were continually being taken away for other tasks. This led to a lack of continuity *and severe reduction of essential services. The necessary interim arrangements to provide child protection for those under 18 years old had been ignored.'*

The released jailbird, whose first brush with the courts had been when he was ten years old, was now a squeaky-clean Christian. His contact with the courts had been almost exclusively as a child under the age of eighteen. He, who had so recently left boyhood, breathed a sigh and got on the mini-bus that was to take him to the station and home to his parents. Because there had been no child protection legislation in 1966, he had been left to sink or swim according to how quick-witted he was able to be in a crisis. He had made allies of the more violent prisoners and officers, and avoided the child abusers. He had thus been lucky to avoid the abusers of his physical body. However, he had not been so fortunate with those who abused his emotional life.

But now, born again in his spirit, he was determined that in the future, in his Christian ministry, he would fight for the protection and defence of children and work with all his energies for the conversion of people to Christ. He would work among the poor and bring relief to prisoners and their families.

This was what lay deep in the heart of the skinny little man who stood at the gates of Rochester Prison that day. What the future would hold, no one knew. He was resolved that it would be different from the past.

It was a short journey to the station. Not a particularly interesting or engaging journey under normal circumstances. However, for him it was a long journey – the longest trip he had taken for nine months; it was the most interesting journey he'd ever made. Even the housing estate and the rubbish-tip looked friendly; little fires dotted about on the dump, with gangs of displaced wanderers casually tending them. A river in the distance, and a caravan site. Ignoring the fact that these were indicators of deprivation and poverty, he afforded himself the luxury of a romantic vision. Otherwise the world was too hard a place.

He ruminated over the letter he had written home a couple of days earlier,

" They tell me you have agreed to have me at home. I don't deserve a home. I'm only glad you have put up with me all this time. I don't know how I shall ever repay you..."

Then apprehension welled up inside him; his stomach muscles tensed, and he found it hard to breathe. He pressed his face against the rear window of the mini-bus.

"Take me back," he whispered, "I want to go back." Desperate to go home, yet his fists were white at the knuckles, clenched and sweating, his soul cried out, "Oh, God. I don't want to go home."

He couldn't face the probation officer, disillusioned and suffering from chronic arthritis after years of impotent powerlessness to really help any of the children in his care, or the family, still resentful of his past behaviour and too poor to feed and clothe him if he didn't get a job, the neighbours whom his father hated and who now had something against him, the Job Centre that had fewer and fewer jobs, with the mounting troubles between the unions and the Labour government, and the creaking welfare system that was even now suffering sharp cutbacks in public spending as a result of the devaluation of the pound under Harold Wilson.

Against all reason he heard himself crying out to his new Friend, Jesus, "Take me back to my cell. I want my cell."

He couldn't face the probation officer, the family, and worst of all, the accusations of his father about what the neighbours thought. His father was a strict disciplinarian who appeared never to have done anything wrong, and whose judgement against most people, criminal or not, this young man had always experienced as harsh, vicious, merciless and crushing.

Despite the way his life had gone thus far, he did not like changes. Alterations, and new faces worried him. He probably feared he'd never fit in anywhere. No one would accept him. Whatever the reason, the fear filled him; what could he do? What would he say? He couldn't go back now. He told himself contrary to the experience of the past three years, it had been all right in the nick. Everyone there had been in the same boat. Prisoners live away from the outside world. They are comfortably oblivious of the fact that beyond the walls, ordinary people walked free, and times changed. Most people in the world were not criminals. People who were confined within four walls in the prison system might laugh about them, deride them, make jokes about them, and call them 'mugs'. Well, it was safe in the nick, and there were no responsibilities. Inside, all necessities for life were provided. Prisoners had to find ways of ameliorating the distress of their situation; of maintaining a 'front' of bravado; of pretending that they were masters of their own destiny. After all, they were in reality owned and controlled by the state through the prison staff that worked a shift system and went home to their working-class families every night.

Outside it was so big. There were so many people. There were so many places to go, yet no-where to go. He remembered suddenly that he actually knew nobody. All his recent contacts, whom he knew so well, were behind him within those four grey walls. Al the people he had known before, in his home town, would be three years older, married, with children or moved from the area, or even dead. Anyway, they had only been school friends, not real friends. They would all be grown-up now.

Who would be there for him? There would be social workers, probation officers, professional care workers of all kinds; people at the Job Centre and the careers office; do-gooders. Did these people really help? They were like the prison guards – they worked their shifts and then went home to their families. And why not? A voice from deep inside shocked and frightened him with what it said, 'You're all alone. Now, not the guards, nor even the criminals are your friends. You have left the frying pan, and now it's the fire. You stand with what little money you have in your pocket and the clothes on your back. That's all. Nothing else.'

The little station at the bottom of the hill on which the prison stood came in to view. He stopped thinking and became interested in what he was seeing. Women with short mini-skirts and young men with long hair. This sounds strange today, when kind wear what they like, so long as it conforms to peer pressure, but forty years ago, this was the beginning of a social and sexual revolution. Two years earlier these young men would have been thought hooligans, simply because of their tribal hair. Now, they seemed to be standard model, conforming young people. To him, it was odd to see them out in the open. Even odder, since for the past three years in prison he had not seen people with long hair, and there were no female prison guards in men's prisons. It would be some years before a female governor reigned in Rochester Prison, for example.

Meanwhile, these longhaired young men had become typical, and it was he, with the short-cropped, prickly scalp, who looked out of place. He had a moment of feeling absurd, and longed briefly for his little cell again. Shuffling quietly to the platform, he settled down on a corner of the bench to wait for the train.

In his pocket was the little money the authorities had taken from him when he was arrested three years ago. There was maybe enough for a packet of cigarettes and some candy. He couldn't remember where the money had come from originally and whether it had been earned or stolen. He took it out and looked down at it. A single note and some coins. Having not handled any actual money for so long, it seemed unreal, like Monopoly money. For a second he had the mad anxiety that it was no longer legal tender. Would the storekeeper refuse to take it?

He sensed that everyone who passed him on the platform looked at him strangely, as though he were a freak. He thought it must be his hair, or perhaps his shabby prison-release suit. 'But', he thought, 'I could be a soldier on leave or demob. The government also clothes soldiers, although it would be the military, not the prison service. The feelings of anxiety would not leave him, and he felt that he must look institutionalised. The pallor of his skin, the smell of his clothes – there is a very special smell that pervaded everything in prison, including the clothes-store. Perhaps it was the shoes, with the heavy studs and thick soles. He wanted to smile at the people as they passed – especially at the girls. Was this not the day of his rejoicing – of celebration? Balloons, a hurdy-gurdy, tickertape and streamers... However, he was afraid that if he smiled, they would laugh. He did not smile, all of the time he stood at the station. As he waited for the train, he slipped into the frame of mind that he was an alien –as he had always felt himself to be since childhood. It was his default emotional position.

It was a 1960's suburban open-plan railway carriage, before the advent of graffiti. There was a single available seat near the door, which increased his uncomfortable self-awareness. Being with strangers in a confined space without the overarching rules that governed prisoners unsettled him and made him feel vulnerable. Other passengers, he thought, would be local people, well aware that he was the latest released from the prison on the hill. At certain times of the year, he ruminated, the gates would be opened, and odds-and-ends of people would shuffle into the sun in their thin suits, big boots and cropped hair, make their way through the town and wait at the station. These would be anonymous people, sticking out like sore thumbs, trying not to be seen, choosing the corners to sit in, rolling thin cigarettes and avoiding glances. Surely, they all knew.

He wanted to cry out, 'God loves me! He knows me inside-out, and still loves me!' But he did not dare. It would have been too much of an admission of vulnerability – like showing your poetry to someone who lacks understanding. No. It couldn't be done. Moreover, what was more, he was not that certain God really loved him.

The loneliness of that journey was almost intolerable. He felt dreadfully alone. His throat was beginning to tickle, and he was terrified of coughing and drawing attention to himself. The last thing he wanted was for people to look up from their papers and magazines. He knew it was irrational, and they couldn't do him any harm. But what if they were to look, and his absurd little figure became the centre of attention. |The cough began to force itself out. He couldn't stop it. He thought that perhaps when he coughed he would re-position himself and stare out of the window, then it wouldn't matter if anyone looked. He coughed gently. Another followed, and another. He dared not move. Normally, with a grin on his face, he would make a joke of it and pass it off with a witticism. He'd have banged his chest with a fist and pretended to be a gorilla to general merriment. He gazed emptily out of the window with the hair on the nape of his neck tingling, longing for the journey to end.

In his pocket was a flimsy form. It was headed,

Prison Act 1952

Notice to a Person Released from a Borstal

It had his name on it, and told him how the Secretary of State had authorised his release from borstal. The form told him about certain commitments he had to keep if he wanted to stay out of borstal. There were six Rules:

You must visit your probation officer when you get home.

He wondered if they had planted someone on the train to make sure he didn't get into any trouble on the way home. It might have been anyone in the carriage. Maybe it was the chap over there...

You must keep in touch with your probation officer and always tell him the truth.

That was the second rule he had to keep. He knew what it meant at a deeper level than the surface. Apart from forcing an oath upon him, it meant he would have to visit his probation officer once a week. If he didn't, he would be packed off to prison again. He had visited him before. A good guy, who had become increasingly embittered over the years as he watched the probation system transform caring officers who believed in the possibility of redemption and change, into cynical agents of social control, inspired by ideas of punishment rather than rehabilitation. The skinny teenager wondered how he could try to be a good, law-abiding citizen when every Wednesday or Friday he would be forced to go to the downtown end of the city, through the huge gate on the main road where everybody knew were the probation offices and courts and holding cells. For six days of the week he would have been able to forget about his past, but once a week he'd be reminded of it, and dragged back to it. Bureaucrats, he reflected, could hand out problems as well as solve them. This second rule had a built-in recidivism-rate.

You must avoid bad company.

Yet, once a week, if he kept Rule Two, he would be meeting all of his former friends at the Probation Office! They would all be there. Sitting in the waiting room, rolling cigarettes, repeating age-old jokes and chatting about their latest crimes and what expectations they had for fines or imprisonment. Conversation would center on the two topics, sex and crime, about which they knew only the worst, and none of the best.

The remaining three rules were about work changing address and a command to contact the Probation Office if help was needed. He smiled wryly at the last one. If he had wanted help, it would have been financial; if it had been financial they'd have wanted to know why. The reason would have been that he had lost his job, and if he had lost his job, it's a sure-fire certainty that the police would be knocking at his door.

So much for the form in his pocket. It represented the just demands of the law. He was afraid of the demands of the law. Not because he feared getting caught, but because the law makes people live by rules, and that, he thought, was inhuman. Why couldn't the law learn a lesson from the Bible? Replace the law with love?

He scratched around in the pocket of his prison suit and rescued a crumpled piece of card. On it was printed,

'A new command I give to you. Love one another. As I have loved you, so love one another.'
Words of Jesus.

The card was in the same pocket as the form. There were fewer words to read, but they were saying much more. They seemed to offer simplicity and hope. They felt unconditionally faithful. He felt that they demanded something of him that he was able, willing, and enthusiastic to give.

The journey ended and there was no difficulty in getting across the city. He took his time, admiring the pretty women along the route. He had been starved of free femininity for three years. It was springtime in the year and in his veins!

He shot a glance backwards to see if he could spot the man from the ministry following him. He knew he was being paranoid, but it had become a habit. Like inadvertently calling every mature male, 'Sir'. He wondered if for the rest of his life he would be looking behind him and submitting himself to every older male.

He did not expect ever to feel that he was completely in the clear, totally free, entirely without blame or to have no guilt attached to him. But here he was, completely free, without handcuffs, free to take whatever direction on the platform he desired, and whichever train he wanted. His previous transport had been a prison van, delivering him to his cellblock. This time it was a British Rail train. It was beautiful. He thought that if it were a dream he wanted it never to end.

He thought back to the first time he had arrived at a prison. He had never seen one before. As a young offender he had been expecting some kind of run-down mansion in the country. A place some lord or other had abandoned because of rats or dry rot. What he had actually seen made him wince. A huge, redbrick prison where real criminals were spending years and years of their time in tiny cells, locked away from the world.

The holes in the walls – were they really windows – criss-crossed with metal bars, each hid a person. A lumbering oaken metal-studded gate loomed up before the tiny prison vehicle, like the jaw of a great animal, ready to eat him...

He had wanted to believe that day was a dream, and that there was nothing to it. But it was true. He had not woken up. He had gone through the whole of his sentence in that frame of mind. All that had happened to him seemed like an endless dream. It was a mad world of echoing buckets and silences and the gut-wrenching stench of human faeces pervading everything. It had been a world in which you kept asking yourself the same question: 'Is this really happening to me?'

The train for Ipswich, Suffolk, left at 11.30 in the morning. He hurried along and just made it. There was an empty compartment.

Study

Ephesians 2:13, 3:12; I Peter 3:18. It is because of the death of Jesus that we can live in close relationship with God. As you read these verses, allow yourself to marvel at what Jesus has done for you. Take time to feel the warm enjoyment that He loves you.

Pray

Look at a map of your region and ask God to increase your desire to pray for the area. Pray for a transformed life for all prisoners who are returning home and for their families. Pray for the mending of relationships among human beings and with God.

TRIALS AND CHARGES

The digital wall clock in the courtroom registered 10.00. He had always wanted to own a clock like that.

One that told the date as well as the time. It was long before the days of digital technology. The room was panelled in some posh wood, like mahogany, and highly polished so that it reflected the people in the room, like a huge all-embracing mirror. The cleaners had come, done their work, and gone. Now the place was filled with the paraphernalia of justice: dusted wigs, polished buttons on the uniforms of the police, and that special smell of cut flowers – like a crematorium, wafting up from the corruption of the remand cells below.

He gazed at the floor in a show of humility. He had seen it on the television. If the head of the court sees that the accused is repentant and humble, she is more likely to have a heart and let him off. It was important for the magistrates to feel powerful. After all, that was why they were in the game. They were sad volunteers who had so little in their lives that they got a thrill from having power over children. That was what he thought, anyway. It had been his experience.

Yes, he gazed at the floor. It was important for them to see that what they had before them was a repentant person, recognising that he had no defence for his crime. Arrogance and having a quick reply would not get him off. It would not be wise to be clever.

His only hope was that humility and repentance would touch the bench's heart.

Although he had signed a confession, it had been under pressure. He could not say what the nature of that 'pressure' was. Partly, he had thought that if he refused to sign they would have put him in a cell for the night. That would have had a number of bad consequences. The worst of these would have been that his vengeful and violent father would discover what his son had been doing. He was a proud and poor working class man. All he had in life was his own tiny domain of power within the family. Threaten that, and you would incur the merciless wrath of the dictator. Life would have been an even worse hell than normal. His father wanted the neighbourhood to believe that he was a respectable and upright man. That was all the respect he had. How could he keep that pretence and maintain the respect of the neighbourhood if one of his sons had become a convicted criminal?

It had not been the fear of physical punishment, not guilt, nor argument that had made Roy sign the confession. It was the dread of the punishment that would ensue if his father found out. His mother would not have minded, because her view about everything relating to her husband was that if she could find ways of frustrating his desire she would do so. She both feared and hated him, and she shared these feelings of hatred and embittered resentment often with this, her favourite son. She was too ignorant and uneducated to realise that this kind of behaviour among parents engendered insecurity and anxiety in the child. He did not know that, either. From his viewpoint, he hated his father and loved his mother. He was bad and she was good. He was angry whereas she was kind, gentle, forgiving, and redeeming.

'Yes, Sir'. Oh, brother, how that 'Sir' stuck in his throat. His name *was* what had been asked. He reckoned it was safe enough to admit that much. 'Yes, Sir.' What else could a bloke say in a room panelled with polished mahogany and filled with brilliant people in wigs? He did do the crime, and he had not been prepared to explain it because it would have uncovered the crimes of some of his friends. He was not a grass.

He wished the walls would fall down. As the talking went on without termination, his mind was diverted. He fantasised that he could go to another country and start all over again. Get born into a rich family and give away trinket on the streets of Rome. In which case he might find himself on the other side of the dock – handing out sentences rather than suffering them. He'd be a good magistrate because he could understand the small-time criminal mind from first hand. Of course, it would have to be done by reincarnation and all that...

' To borstal...'

The word brought him back to the dock, the courtroom, and the town of Ipswich in Suffolk. They were actually going to do it! His mind spun into delirious action with images of short haircuts and unavailable friends mingling with thoughts of injustice, punishment and a feeling of acute self-pity.

His official criminal record had begun at twelve years old, although his criminal activity had been going on long before then. He could not remember a time when he had not been a thief and a liar. But by twelve years old he had been sentenced at the Juvenile Court to three twelve-month probation orders for larceny. Then, at seventeen he was given a fine and a disqualification from driving. Four months later, he was sentenced to three terms of probation for three years for auto crimes and for driving whilst disqualified. Today was eighteen months later. What would be the decision of the Quarter Sessions Court?

'On the charge of housebreaking and stealing, you are to be given borstal training for three years. On the charge of driving whilst disqualified you are to be given a period of three years borstal training. On the charge of taking and driving away a motor vehicle you are to be given a period of three years borstal training. On the charge of driving without insurance you are to be given a period of three years borstal training. On the charge of driving whilst disqualified for the second time, you are to be given a period of three years borstal training...'

His mind reeled. Fifteen years prison? Surely not. Not fifteen years. He'd be an old man by the time he got out of prison...

' However, this is not all. You are due to appear at Kings Lynn Magistrates Court on 27th May 1965 to face charges of larceny, aiding and abetting taking and driving away a motor vehicle on two occasions and of aiding and abetting driving with no licence and no insurance. You will no doubt be given other sentences if you are found guilty of these offences. This will mean that you will have to attend the courts from whatever Borstal Institution you are placed in at the time. Have you anything to say?'

To say? Say what? He could not speak, let alone put some words together into a coherent sentence.

'Take him down!'

The police officer grabbed the eight-and-a-half stone criminal by the arm. He was unable to speak and suddenly needed a lavatory. The burly policeman's hand went round the lad's skinny wrist and escorted him down the cold stone steps – worn in the middle – where generations of captive feet had climbed for many years to have their fortunes told, and retreated with their heavy loads. Each step had an echo of its own. He passed by several statues of local worthies who had deciphered hieroglyphics, found a way to get from the middle of Africa to the Mediterranean, or discovered some drug or other. Their grey stone busts sat atop marble columns and frowned mercilessly down upon him as he made his way to the cells. Mahogany banister rails, smelling of beeswax shone in the dim lamplight.

He wondered if the magistrates had already begun to wonder about the job they had just done. Surely the echo of the stone steps must make them do a rethink...

They led him down to the cells. An odd smell seeped across the corridor. It was a smell he was to become accustomed to in the years ahead. It was the combination of stone walls, gloss paint, the shed cells of the unwashed human body, and faeces left sweating in tin chamber pots in the open air.

The prisoner wears the same clothes as all the others who preceded him in that place. He becomes anonymous. The prison cell is the locus of his every activity. He eats all his meals and sleeps all his slumbers in it. He scrubs the wooden floor from wall to wall with a special scrubbing brush made by the female prisoners in a neighbouring penal establishment, so that the scrubbing brush becomes a symbol of unity, kinship, and connection.

The difference between a prison cell and a police cell is the smell of the smoke in the wood and brick. In a police cell the smell is thick and sickly. This is because the prisoners smoke civilian, ready-made cigarettes that have more tar in them. These are cigarettes left over from civvy-street. But in a prison, no one can afford civilian ready-made cigarettes. The smell is of sharp, harsh and strong Black Shag.

It was hard for him to believe that all those people had got their heads together and stuck him away in a little room all on his own. Was this what it all came down to in the end? One room for one man; the result of all that vast and complex structure and machinery of the law. It was hard to believe that this was the end result of so respected and feared an institution. It was the first example he had come across of an ideal in action. Such a tremendous disparity.

The door of the cell was thick and looked very heavy. It was reinforced with steel and concrete and heavy bars and bolts. In the centre, about a third of the way down was a small, round thickened glass window. The glass distorted the image on the other side.

It reminded him of when he was a little boy. He had done something wrong, stayed off school or something. They had been very angry with him and banged him around the head and ears. He had tried to say he was sorry and wouldn't do it again. He had tried to say it wasn't fair and that it had not been intentional.

He had wanted to say that he did it because he couldn't help it. He wanted them to pick him up and cuddle him and make it better, to give him comfort and reassurance. But they never had. And he could think of no good reason why they should. After all, he was bad. He had felt helpless.

Thrown on their mercy, he had been cast away. Though he had needed them, they had not needed him. So he submitted himself to their merciless punishment. When it was over he felt that he had suffered in order to satisfy the just demands of the ones he loved. They had sent him off to the bedroom and locked him away on his own. He had wanted to go and play with the other kids in the street. He could hear them playing outside, but there he was, an alien starting to experience his life destiny.

Over the years, the love he had for his family began to turn to resentment and loathing. At first, all he had wanted to do was show them that he loved them. It had now come to the point, at seventeen, where all he wanted to do was escape from them, to get away from their world, and to start a life of his own. If it meant going to prison, then so it must be. At least, that was his reasoning, and it was, after all, his life.

Feeling the same loathing and hatred, locked away in a small smelly room yet again, and again, afraid to cry out for fear of the consequences – he had heard about what they do to troublemakers – he aimed his concentrated hatred toward the door. He wanted the lavatory, and putting his ear to the tiny glass window could hear female voices echoing down the corridors.

The magistrates were going home. He hung on. He would have to wait until things got less busy outside before making a fuss. His eyes wandered around the cell. On the walls were all kinds of lewd scrawling. He wondered if anyone had been caught doing graffiti on the cell wall and punished for it. Then, the sound of keys and echoing boot-falls. He wondered what it was that motivated prison guards and policemen. It must take some strange kind of mentality to enjoy keeping human being locked up like rabbits.

' Right, lad, lets have your braces, belt, shoelaces and tie. Come on. Get a move on I aint got all day. Don't worry about that, you can pull your trousers up when I've got your things. Come on, come on. Shoelaces? Well, break the knots then. Right. Got a watch on? No? Right.'

Bang!

Tinkle, tinkle, tinkle diminished as he walked away from the door down the corridor. He could not have helped seeing the prisoner's shabby underwear with the holes in. He had said it all without moving his mouth. It was a ritual; as though it was something he did every day. This was not personal; it was like the charnel house or the chicken-farm. People not cows, human beings not fowl. People walked overhead. He could hear their muffled voices and music in the distance.

He had been given no indication of how long he was to be held in the cells under the courtrooms. In the end, it did not make much difference, he reasoned. He had been given three years to serve, and what did it matter where he served it. His series of three-year sentences had, mercifully, to run concurrently, not consecutively as he had at this time feared. It might as well be here. Three hours of his three-year sentence had now been served.

Contrary to his hope and expectation that being a prisoner might be exciting and romantic, actually it was frightening, boring and stultifying. Nothing was happening. He dampened the end of a stub of pencil and scratched on the wall,

'The quality of mercy is not strain'd –
It droppeth as the gentle rain from heaven
Upon the place beneath: it is twice blest –
It blesseth him that gives, and him that takes...'

Yes, this uneducated prisoner knew Shakespeare. He had spent much of his time learning how to become a human being through study of these works. Others might think this was pathetic. What a laugh! A working class delinquent scribbling Shakespeare on the wall of his cell. But he had meant it. Perhaps, he fantasised, the magistrate may come in here one day, read what was written, and have a moment of reflection about the work he does each day. It may lead to a change of heart. Of course no one would believe the skinny prisoner who enjoyed driving cars without a licence had written it there, of even if he had written it, that he had understood it.

This, and much more occurred to him while he waited in the holding-cell. This was the first cell of his prison and borstal career. Some of the things he thought that day were not true; he knew that he was being vindictive. But how else was he to face the fact that he'd committed a series of crimes and was now, according to the due process of the law, beginning to have his punishment. It was hard for him to realise that it was himself who was going through this process, and not some fictional character in a book. Up until now, everything that happened, happened to someone else, and he had always been an onlooker.

Clonk clonk clonk. Tinkle tinkle, squeak 'Right. Get up. Get these on.' Click. Handcuffs! He was flattered. The glamour faded a bit when the police officer said,

'Sorry lad. Got to put these on. Regulations, see.'

The skinny prisoner thought, as they led him along the corridor, that the thought of escape could not have been further from his mind. Along with six other prisoners, sentenced that day, he was led single-file across the narrow strip of freedom that lay between the building and the prison van. The men were then taken to the police station downtown, and then to a police car and off to the first of the many prisons and borstals that were to follow.

He had been given to understand that he was being taken to a remand home. He tried to imagine what this would be like as they sped towards Norwich, fifty miles north of Ipswich, which was their destination. At age eleven he had been taken in to care of the social services after the attempted suicide of his mother. It had been a large redbrick building in the center of town. During the many months that he was there, he had made some friends, and a special girlfriend with whom he had fallen in love. He thought that maybe the remand home would be something like that. Anyway, he was not overly anxious about it. He had been through the worst.

On reaching the city of Norwich, the car turned a corner and a tall red brick wall barred the way. Along the top of the wall ran a slippery, grey ceramic capping, topped with curled razor wire. He looked blankly at the wall, and the huge, studded double gates. Surely they had taken a wrong turning and gone down a cul de sac. But the grey wall that rose behind the red brick wall had regular small square windows in it. These were cross-crossed with bars and metal slats. This was Norwich Prison. It was not a remand home. The skinny prisoner was to spend some eventful months in Norwich Prison. It would be his baptism into the criminal justice punishment system.

After driving across the yard he was led through a barred door into a small office. A long coconut-matting runner led from the office to the reception annexe. He was ordered to undress and have a bath. The bathroom had no door. The smell of carbolic hit his senses. That, and urine. A scrubbed hard slatted board ran along the bathroom floor, and a well-work rough towel hung on a peg in the wall. The procedure was to ensure that new prisoners had no communicable diseases or parasites, and that there were no hidden drugs being brought in.

A thorough search was necessary before any new person was allowed to enter that hallowed place of rationed tobacco and cartel controlled drugs. He was slightly embarrassed, and it was necessary to cast off some individuality in order to handle the situation. He became suspicious of the officer who insisted on chatting to him while he had his bath. Was he gay? He couldn't say. What were the ethics in this place? He had heard of other prisoners being raped and abused by other prisoners. Might it happen between guards and prisoners as well? He didn't know, and so he hastened his bath, while maintaining as much of his modesty as he was able. He clambered into his oversized prison clothes as hastily as possible. They stank, and were rough and hard. They were too big. Others were too small. Some had holes. They could have had large arrows and 'W.D.' printed on them and it would not have seemed out of place. As it was, he was glad to get anything on, and out from under the gaze of the bathroom guard.

They took him to a cell and locked him in. He sat on the floor among the misshapen clothes and cried.

The day was over.

Study

Romans 5:8; 1 Timothy 1:15. Christ loved us and saved us when we weren't interested in him. His love is amazing. He loves you today regardless of how you feel about yourself. This is good news.

Pray

Pray for the major cities in your region and for young people especially who are coming before the courts. Pray for their hearts to find true love in Jesus.

Pray for their homes and communities to be transformed.

AUTO THEFT

There had been generations of gloss paint on the brick walls of those cells. Paint was peeling off the paint that had been painted over the paint. It mocked him as he entered the cell, reminding him of the cool nights after hot scorching days in the sun, when he could relax, stripping tiny bits of burned skin off his arms. The cell was hot and dank. In the far corner a pot stank; the last person to scrub the wooden floor had scrubbed around it, and it sat in its own dark circle. Two parallel bars ran three inches from the wall near the floor. It was part of the heating system. In the wall at the far end of the cage, two thirds of the way up and four feet out of reach at about four metres up was a window, appearing to have been cut out of the solid concrete.

Three slanted cast iron slats ran across the window-space outside and inside there were sixteen small, thickened glass window-squares. It occurred to him that the object of a window was twofold: one, to let in the light, and two, to afford the occupant of the room a view through the wall to what lies beyond. This contraption made a poor job of both. Each small square had a cast-iron frame, so it had the feel more of a cast iron object than a glass one.

The floor consisted of badly fitting wooden planks. The dusty, naked bulb, five metres up bathed them in an eerie green light. There was a wooden Ercol schoolroom chair. He remembered having a chair like that where he was at his first school, only half the size. From another corner of the cell a block of scrubbed wood stuck out. It was a table. There was no bed, so that he wondered if he was expected to sleep on the floor. He did not know, really, whether people in prison slept at all. He supposed they must!

He had finished crying and had got round to swearing about all the rotten things the world had prepared for him. He kicked the pot and it rang round the room, skidding across the floor, the lid falling off in the process and resting its rim jauntily against the wall. He left it there. If they expected him to use that, they were mistaken. He wanted a cigarette. They had taken away all of his personal belongings at reception. He'd had to sign for them. They then wrapped them all in a brown manila envelope and stuck it down with tape.

Prison guards, he ruminated. They must be lacking something emotionally or socially. What sort of people were they? Maybe, he thought, they were bossed around by their wives and violent towards their children. They came to work to take it out on the prisoners. They had been after him since he was ten years old. He brooded on the thought of all those grown-up policemen keeping files on a child of ten so they could nab him when he got ripe at seventeen. That, at least, was how it seemed to him.

He sat on the top bar of central heating and got burned. He cursed. He climbed up on to the chair and opened the two tiny moveable squares of glass. The chair wobbled and he crashed to the floor in a fuming heap. He wanted a cigarette. He wanted to use the lavatory, and he wanted to be let out of that lonely little cell.

Frightened what might result, he nevertheless pressed the alarm bell in the wall by the door.

A warder poked his eye into the little round hole in the door.

'Shut up, git!'

'Please. Sir, I want a pee'.

'Look, you'll get out of here when I'm good and ready, see. Now shut up. Any more trouble from you and I'll keep you locked up all the longer. I'm a busy man. There's two hundred more of you out here. I'm not a wet nurse. Do you realise if I let everyone out who wanted a pee, I would be at it all night. I'm a man on my own, and I don't get paid for all the crap I get...'

'Click'. The metal cover swung freely back and forth over the spy hole. The sound of keys and studded boot steps clanking on the metal gantry floor faded gradually in to the distance. This is what was to pass for a social life for the skinny prisoner for the next few months in holding-prison prior to allocation prison prior to being given a borstal where, in theory the 'training' would begin. He felt like a little human machine.

It was going to be a strange relationship between an anonymous warder who spoke through a hole in the door when on duty and in the mood to talk, and a skinny teenager starving desperately for any kind of human contact, whether it happened to be his jailer or his saviour. Was there more than a pay cheque at the end of the month for him? Was he a carer, or just a prison guard? Did he have a heart? Was there a soul in his body? Did he have a family? Were they pleased to see him when he came home at night? Did his little kids run to him and jump up for a cuddle, or did they hear his footsteps in the drive and run and hide, not knowing what mood he would be in tonight?

What sort of social life do prison guards have? Do they have a life at all? Maybe they go down the club at night and get drunk. And what sort of psychological effect does their job have on them. A deep one, probably. It must be so, thought the skinny boy, for how could a man treat his follow human beings like caged animals every day and then go home and be normal? And he had called him, 'Sir'.

It was a sad thing when a bloke was prepared to sell his human dignity for a chance to go to the lavatory, it would have been better to use the pot. He was angry because he had to *ask*. Despite the warder, despite himself, he got the pot and used it. It was to be the first of many thousands of times. The pot rang and he was afraid the warder would return and poke his eye in the hole again. The pot and the water jug both had little green bumps of lime encrustations on them. The health implications of this prison cell did not bear thinking about.

He stood there thinking of all the people without faces who had contributed towards his being put there. They – he was sure – were the people with all the money. They were the ones who were successful in hiding their dirt under the carpet. It seemed to him that he was also their dirt. The scum of the earth. The offscouring of everything. The truth, it seemed to him, was that he had got all the problems and for all their so-called cleverness, they did not have the solutions. So what did they do? The shut the problems away in little cages, doled out a bit of grub from time to time to ease their consciences and paid sadists to keep the problems hidden away. He wondered whether the whole thing was a living picture of what went on their own minds with their own problems. Did they deal with them also by pretending that they didn't exist, repressing them, and locking them away out of sight? He wondered how many powerful people were really sick little weaklings besieged by their own fears and fantasies about themselves.

He sank to the floor in the corner for comfort and closed his eyes. He had never thought these things before. Did this bode what the future would hold.

Before today he had thought only what he wanted to put in his mouth. Now, after just one day, he had started to think about life... The best thing was to go to sleep, whatever dreams may come. Not too much, though. He didn't know if sleeping was allowed this early in the evening. An old battered Bible lay on the table. It had the word, 'Gideons' printed on it. He drifted off to sleep, wondering what Gideon had done to get put inside, whether he'd been released yet, and whether he'd been caught again, and what would happen tomorrow.

Over the months that were to follow he was to discover that sleeping would be his major pastime. He was to discover that he could hone the art of dropping off to sleep at a moments notice and in any situation; whether on the lavatory or at the dining table. When he slept, he dreamed. The first sleep of his prison career was a nightmare – only it happened in the daytime.

He began to hear the sound of motorbikes and laughter, and it all flooded back. A picture of the Plough Inn, in Ipswich, his hometown came to his mind. It was July and hot, about two months before his arrest and sentence to prison. He was chatting with some of his friends outside the Plough. They had been drinking, and there had been some girls around. Jack was busy shouting his mouth off about how he could do eighty on his new scooter – maybe even ninety if it was downhill.

A group of girls stood around, hero-worshipping. If he could do ninety, so could the skinny teenager. The only problem was he didn't have a scooter to prove it. It was amazing what sex appeal a motorbike had. The girls seemed to flock around the Fonz, even though in this case Fonz was a Suffolk hillbilly. The skinny teenager was mad. What a stupid way to measure the worth of a man 'Has he got a motorbike?' But since this *was* their way of telling, he decided he had no choice but to go along with it.

' Jack. Let me have your bike.'

' You must be joking. You're not insured and you haven't got a licence. How do I know you can even ride it anyway? '

' Afraid I could do ninety on it, are you?'

Jack decided the only way to defend his position in the eyes of those present was either to do ninety himself, or let me have a go.

'Aw, come on Jack. Just a little ride up the road. I won't be a minute. Just up the road and back. I bet I can do ninety.'

By this time everyone had joined in; some on Jack's side – the more law-abiding ones, and the majority on his.

' Go on, Jack. Let him see if he can do ninety on it.'

' Yeah. Go on, Jack. You're not *chicken* are you?'

Knowing the importance of that last challenge, Jack wavered. In a final desperate attempt to avoid having his new scooter wrecked – because that was what most of the group expected to happen – he brought out his trump card.

'And what if he comes off it, then, eh? How am I going to explain to the police and the insurance company? If I say I let him ride it, they won't pay me anything, and I'll be in trouble for aiding and abetting a crime.'

But the skinny teenager had a better card. One that would make him a hero as well as the winner of this particular game.

'I'll tell you what, Jack. If I come off, which is unlikely, because I reckon I'm pretty good on bikes, I'll give the police the wrong name and address and let them think I've stolen it. That way, you'll be in the clear, your insurance company will pay out, and they won't have anything to go on. All you have to say is someone pinched your bike. I'll shoot off and get clear, and everything'll be rosy. Anyway, I won't come off, will I now Jack?'

In a last desperate poor Jack decided to ask for some money to cover the cost of the fuel. The skinny teenaged handed him a note and mounted the bike. He had won.

After a few false starts, he had powered off down the street on full throttle. It had never seriously occurred to him that he would have an accident. He was young, and life was eternal. It was other people who died. Prestige. Respect. That was important. All the girls and all of his mates had watched him negotiate the bike-ride, and every one of them would in future be aware that he was a hero for offering to take any blame.

With respect, you can take liberties with people. They get to thinking you are doing them a favour when really you're exploiting them. What a laugh. In future he would have sufficient respect to borrow Jack's bike any time there were mates or girls around. Great stuff. Another Catchpole victory!

Hold on. Whassat? The damn thing began to wobble and buck all over the road. He couldn't control it. The wheels wouldn't hold. For some reason he gave the throttle a twist in the hope that increased speed would help. The bike began to pick up speed. He got scared and jammed the brakes on. The speedometer flashed in to view and it read 60 – only 60? Trees and lamp standards flashed past and the side of the road snaked into the line of his front wheel. Drain covers flashed by, under the wheel as he screamed across the road directly in line of a fuel tanker lumbering up the road. His mind whizzed into action.

A choice had to be made. Whether to hit the tanker wrap himself around a tree trunk or just lay the speeding bike gently on its side and hope for some protection from the faring. He chose the last option. The bike, by this time was doing fifty, veered onto its side, and using the scooter as a shield, he kept his head down, hands off the grips, leaning over, gently – right, here it comes...

'*Bang!*' seems such a tame word to describe what happened next. It wasn't a bang or a crash. It was more of a deep concentration, like the mainspring of a tightly-wound clock forcing itself to unwind inside your head, and the only thing you can utter is a kind of profound, Arrrrrrrrrrrrrrrrrrrrrgh between your clenched jaws. Then it stops. Silence for a few seconds.

Then consciousness returns. You look down at your trousers and discover a neat little red hole in each leg. Then the pain in your arms begins and when you look you see two neat red holes in the cuffs of your new coat. It's all over in no time at all, and you begin to wonder what all the fuss was about. It was only an accident.

It was some minutes before he remembered why he had been so anxious. The police! He must get away before they arrived. Otherwise there would be all hell to pay. He couldn't hang around. They would want to see his licence and insurance. He had already promised Jack he would take the blame for stealing the vehicle and he couldn't go back on that. His leg and arm hurt. He thought he must have grazed it on the road surface. He began to get up, but found that he couldn't walk. No wonder – he was shaking like a leaf. He cursed himself for getting so scared he couldn't stand. Then there was this fussy woman interfering with him.

("Get off, you stupid woman. Get your hands off me.")

'Thank you, ma'am. You're very kind. Yes, I'm perfectly OK thank you. No, not at all. Thank you very much for trying to help. I'm very grateful, ma'am.'

(Why don't you get off, woman? Leave me alone. Oh, hell, if she keeps hanging on to me like this, the police will be here in a minute and then I'll be deep in it.)

He pulled himself away from the woman's motherly clutches and tried to make it up the street. His legs wouldn't carry him.

'Come inside and have a cup of tea.'
He gave up and resigned himself to the kind woman's ministrations. Her kindly face told him a tale he didn't want to hear but could do nothing about. The police were on their way. He couldn't escape. He was well and truly caught.

'Come on, I'll clean you up a bit.'

He nodded. There was nothing else he could do. Oh, well, what will be will be and all that. The woman had telephoned the police service, trying to be helpful. She had a go at removing his trousers while he tried desperately to keep them on without wanting her to realise that he was embarrassed.

'Look, ma'am if you really want to help, don't you think it would be better to wait for the police, or the ambulance, they're trained for this sort of thing.'

'It's OK. I'm a nurse.'

He was caught, and resigned himself to her first aid care.

It wasn't long before the friendly neighbourhood police arrived.

'Ello sir. Got a bump then 'ave you?'

'It's nothing, officer. I just fell of my bike. A bit wet, you know. You know how dodgy it can be in the wet. Wish I'd never *bought* the damn thing now!'

'*Bought it* then, did you, sir? In both senses of the word, then.'

He chucked at his own joke.

'Hurt, then, are you?'

'Nope. Just a scratch. This nice lady is a nurse and she's sorting me out.'

'Yes. Got a licence have you?'

'Yes, thank you, officer. It's at home though. I'll get off home as soon as it's sorted out and get the bike fixed. It's just got a bit of a dent, I think.

' So I couldn't actually *see* your licence, then, could I sir?'

'Well, yes. As I say, I keep it at home. It's a bit silly carrying it around with me, I always think. I don't think I have it on me, though. Perhaps I do.'

He fumbled around a bit, making it look as though he was expecting to find it any minute.

'Nope. Afraid I've left it at home. (Look a bit groggy, as though you can't think quite straight yet.

The result of the accident.) 'This leg hurts a bit. I had better get home and rest it as soon as possible, I think.

'Insurance at home as well, then, I expect, is it?'

He nodded.

'Where do you live?'

He gave a false address and name. The officer turned to his partner and asked him to get on the phone and check it out. He was done for.

'Right. Now we'll have you proper name and your proper address and whether or not this bike is yours or if you've nicked it, shall we? Name?'

'Roy catchpole.'

'Address.'

'103 Spenser Road.' The roads on his corporation estate were named for famous British writers and poets.

'Right. Come with me.'

'What about my leg?'

'Stuff yer leg.'

The police station was small and echoing. Uniformed officers busily engaged over typewriters and huge mugs of tea peopled the stuffy atmosphere. A black-stockinged woman hurried by, arms filled with files. There was a whiff of canteen coffee, and odds and ends of people sat in various attitudes propped against the wall on a long bench. He was whisked past the desk and escorted to the rear of the building. Cells.

'Here. You're not putting me in a *cell*!'

A very heavy-witted policeman said, 'Tell yer what, lad. We'll give you a key and have a telly brought in from the electrical shop of you like. How would that suit you? You can come and go, as you like then. How would you like that?

As it turned out, he told them everything they wanted to know. Only he did say that he had stolen the scooter, and it made him feel good to have shown that bit of loyalty to his friend. At about ten that night, they let him go home. He wandered homeward, trousers flapping in the cold evening air and his best jacket torn beyond repair. It was a dark night and he walked through the town. Past the Quick Snax, the cafes, the prostitutes and the cheap neon town-fronts that waited for the daytime town to go to sleep before it opened up its eyes for the nightly fun. Past the big mouths and the alcoholics and the deserted bus stops. Couples kissing in shadowed doorways and empty roads. He was as depressed and sad as hell. It would be difficult getting in to the house without his father finding out. He would have to go through the lavatory window as usual. He couldn't face him that night.

A car drew alongside him, and he got in. It was Gerald Cattermole, a carpenter. He would have cause to remember that night when a carpenter picked him up when he was feeling low. Gerald lived just up the road from his house.

'Here Roy mate. What's up?'

'Nothing. Fell over.'

Study

John 14:16; 1 Timothy 2:2. The Bible is very clear that there is only one way that we can fully know God and that is through Jesus Christ. Are there other people or activities that you use to try to approach God? Search your heart now.

Pray

Watch the news for your area today. Vandalism, car theft, larceny from stores and offices, housebreaking, street violence, drug misuse and binge drinking. These are signs of a lost generation of young people. Pray for these people of your community.

ANGER MANAGEMENT

It was four in the afternoon when they unlocked him. The door swung open quietly and easily on its heavy greased hinges and he got to his feet. An overweight warder bawled out to follow him. He wondered if they were taking him off for another bath – he could have done with one after that cell. Still, he could not help thinking it would have been better to clean the cell. They were not, in fact, making for the bathhouse. He was following along a lengthy corridor. The enamelled brickwork shone and reflected the two dull bodies marching purposefully along. One was short and skinny, and the other dumpy and fat. Laurel and Hardy, he thought.

The floor red tiled floor was highly polished. It was clearly something the prisoners were given to do every day. At the end of the corridor was a huge barred door: five slim metal bars from the ceiling to the floor and a single flat bar across the middle. The right side carried a huge metal lock.

The fat guard slid one of his keys in to the lock. The sound of keys jangling was to be a constant refrain accompanying almost every activity he was to be involved in for the next three years. The odd pair went through the gate. It rattled shut. A prison within a prison. What he saw before him made him catch his breath. There, right in front of him, was a prison. The actual inside of a real prison. Not something on the TV or in a book or slide show. A real, live, prison, with real live prisoners walking around. Not counting the bottom floor there were three tiers of cast iron webbed walkways running straight from this end of the huge empty space to the other end, about seven hundred yards away. The walkways gave access to hundreds of steel doors, about ten feet apart in the wall, each with a tiny hole at eye level.

Above the ground floor, at ceiling height hung a wire mesh across the hall-space, like the safety net across a circus ring, along the whole length of the prison. All along the four floors dozens of studded doors hung half-hidden in the brick recesses. All the same, except for the number attached to each. In front of him, on the floor, stretched into the distance, a vast area of red ceramic tiling, mirror-polished. At the far end of the interior of the prison – which was one vast room the size of half a dozen aircraft hangers – was another brick wall but with no door in it. It was vast and empty and, apart from the slippered footfalls of one or two prisoners scuttling here-and-there on various errands, entirely silent. Reach tiny sound echoes, and you really could have heard a pin drop.

He was led, subdued, to a chair in the centre of the space, where he was ordered to sit down. He was alone apart from the fat guard. Another guard, with a different uniform on, approached. He grabbed the skinny prisoner by the hair and said,

'Nice hair.'

Not knowing what to expect, he prepared himself for unspeakable torture. He was afraid he would shout and let everyone know he was a coward. The man, brandishing his scissors, set to work on his hair. He hacked and slashed and scraped until there was nothing left but a hairless egg. The hair had been his pride and joy – one of the marks of his rebellion against the rest of the world, his family and the universe of authority. Among his peer group, it had marked him out as someone special. Few of the others had the courage to reject their parents' rules about behaviour and dress, but the skinny prisoner had ignored them all. He went where he wanted to go and did what he wanted to do. At least, that had been his self-assessment. It was not necessarily how others saw him. The hair had taken him years to get right, and now it was being torn from his skull, leaving him naked, cold and exposed. No one could tell how it would affect him. There was no mirror for him the check it out. He felt that it was yet another of the system's ways of destroying him, breaking down his resistance. Like stripping him off in reception, and like the guard watching him bathing, and like leaving him alone in the cell without a bed and without an explanation. Sitting in the prison chair with the convict Trustee cutting his hair, he felt the time had come for him to be ripped apart and have his individuality and uniqueness stripped away. He would have to find another way of identifying himself to himself, and of flagging it to others. He had a made moment of fear that this could signal the beginning of the rest of his life. A life of crime, depravity, degradation and vice, in which there would never be a moment of peace. He would always be hounded by the police and penned-in with criminals. Without the freedom to make choices about what he wanted to do, his actions would be destined by the police and the courts and probation officers and would be against his will. He would no longer be able to do what he wanted to do. The removal of his hair was a sign of his defeat and a predictive indication of the kind of future he could expect. He would be apprenticed to the insane, changed into a criminal, and spewed into the sewers of society, labelled, 'copper-fodder'.

As the hair came off, so his mind raced in a flurry of reflection and decision, casting-off what had been and reaching out for what might be in the future. At the centre of his being was a little altar on which was a candle of survival. If one life was ended, then the next step was not death of the self but the beginning of a new creation. He sat defiantly considering his sentence. Nine months to three years! That was nothing. He was sure he could do that much time without any difficulty. After all, what was nine months? He did not think for a second that in fact, it would be three whole years before he tasted freedom once again.

The barber finished cutting the prisoner's hair, which lay in a heap on the floor. He was tempted to lift his hand to feel how much had been left intact, but he resisted. The guard might take offence and impose a punishment. He gathered from the conversation between guard and trustee that the trustee was himself a prisoner. Because of his closeness to the guard and his contempt for the victim, the skinny prisoner felt further alienated. Little hair had been left, the trustee being on the side of the guard. At that moment he realised something he had not understood before and would never forget. Allegiance was a tool to be used and not an emotion to be felt. He decided to remember that. Another prisoner shuffled by.

'Evening, Bill'

'Evening', replied the guard, 'How is your back?'

'Oh, not so bad today. Yours?'

'Mmmm'.

'You seen officer Jones?'

'Yup. He's about somewhere. He was in the quad when I last saw him. I think he'd been doing Reception. Hang on, there he is now.'

The door at the end of the hall rattled open and along came officer Jones, the Chief Officer. The prisoner hurried off, his buckets of tea clanking and slopping as he went.

'Evening, sir', said the officer, licking the Chief's boots. 'Got a new un here for you. Anywhere in particular you want him?'

'Put him in twelve, floor two.'

'Well, he's all done. I'll bang him up now.'

The prisoner tensed. 'Bang him up'? He wondered what they had in mind. Were they going to give him a beating? He had heard about prison, and now here he was all on his own with no one to report what was happening. There was no way of escape, and it was futile anyway. This whole system is entirely enclosed. If they chose, they could do anything they wanted to do, and no one would know. The child came out and admitted what he was,

'Please, mister, don't beat me up. I won't be any trouble. Just put me away if you've got to. I won't make any noise...'

The fat guard grinned and said,

'Don't worry, kid. Nothing is going to happen to you. 'Bang him up' means 'put him in a cell', that's all. When you put someone in a cell, you bang the door shut. That's all, and it's what I'm going to do for you right now. Come on. Grab your bed and follow me.'

He followed, climbing the cast iron stairway to the second landing. The guard opened the door of the cell that was to be the prisoner's home for the next six weeks. He knew he would have to settle down and wait six weeks until the time came for the first of a series of transfers through the system. In his cell, he sat on the wooden chair and felt his head. The hair had been cropped to the skin, and for the first time he was glad he was somewhere none of his friends could see him. Had he been in town, he would have been humiliated, but here in the prison, it seemed somehow right – as though it was something to be expected. The problem was that for six weeks there would be nothing for him to do. The cell had no games or things to occupy the mind. There was one book, a Bible.

His cigarettes had been taken away at reception, so he couldn't have a cigarette. By the time 17.30 arrived, he had slept fitfully, and was now standing at the window on a small, scrubbed three-cornered table with three legs. There had been a large cup of cold tea on the table, which he had drunk greedily. The nights were getting earlier as winter approached. He banged the cup gently for company and to fill the silence. Before long, he'd got to counting the bricks in the walls, the bars across the window and the gaps between the floor boards. He counted the windows many times, sometimes starting at the top right-hand corner and working down, and other time from the bottom left-hand corner diagonally and them across the top and down, and every possible combination of lines. He counted the chips out of the paint on the door, the cracks in the arched ceiling, the grain-lines in the floor boards and the strands of the cobweb outside the window-slats, blowing fitfully in the breath of air that fondled the stark, rude prison wall. He picked the dirt out from between the floorboards with his fingernails.

He sang some songs gently under his breath and recited some poetry. He drummed his fingers on the table, singing some popular songs and tapping his feet on the floor to keep time. He got up and stretched. He did some push-ups. He got on the chair again and tried to reach up to see out of the window. It was a long way from the floor. He could just see the large open space of heath land outside the window beyond the wall. There were dogs running around and people walking and talking. Some patches of mist hung around on the ground and it was beginning to get dark.

Nearer to the window was a very high wall. Red brick with broken bottle pieces on top of it. At the foot of the wall was a little old man grubbing in the earth. A gardener-convict. He recalled a story he had been mockingly told by a police officer in the Station at Ipswich. How to escape from prison. First, you stand in your cell and shout until you get hoarse, then you jump on the horse and ride until your butt gets sore, then you take the saw and cut the bars and stand by the wall, put the two halves together so you get a whole, put the hole in the wall, jump through, get on the horse and ride to freedom. This was the level of communication he was to expect to have to live with for the next number of years. He would have to make the most of it, and to find ways of entertaining and engaging himself without relying on the system to provide it.

Bored? He was already bored, and the first day had not yet ended!

Some time later in the evening he heard the sound of keys jangling at the far end of the gantry. The sound came closer and closer until the guard stood outside his cell. He heard the sound of muffled voices, but the guard and Trustee with the bucket of tea moved on without opening his door. In his boredom, anger and frustration, deprived of this little bit of human contact he threw himself across the cell, landing awkwardly on the metal bed-frame. A sharp pain shot through his calf, and he smashed the floor with a fist. Without being conscious of it, he was screaming at the top of his voice to have the door opened. At full emotional tilt he raged against the wall, the brick and the hundred layers of gloss paint, hitting again and again with his clenched fist without feeling any pain. The blood might have belonged to someone else. Tears of rage and impotent frustration coursed down his face and he felt nothing but a deep and abiding anger. It tore at his heart and soul and embedded itself in the deepest part of his psyche. When he had finished, noticing the blood, he cuddled his hand in a handkerchief and wiped the red from the wall. The bones of the knuckles gleamed white through the skin. Although the anger had subdued, and he was weeping gently, this reminder of the experience of abandonment had dumped him back on the original shores of his childhood, which had also been lonely and abandoned.

'They missed me. They missed me. It's the same old story. I'm always being missed. Never been noticed.'

He wondered if anyone at home had noticed that he was no longer there. He had often spent days away from home. Either he had lacked the courage to tell anyone in the family that he was due to come to court that morning. Either that, or he had felt that no one would be sympathetic if he shared his deep sadness and anxiety about the world and his place in it. Whatever the case, no one knew. It would not be until they read the newspaper in the morning that they would find out. He knew what they would say. He didn't think they would care much. They would probably be glad to get rid of him. He had always caused them a lot of trouble and worry. His father in particular had suffered whenever the police came to the house. His image of himself was that he was a good, respectable man living in the middle of a very rough corporation estate –

trailer trash people. According to his vision of himself, he was a poor and persecuted human being who had never been given the opportunity to fulfil his academic potential. He was embittered, angry and vengeful, unwilling to talk to any of the neighbours, thinking himself as better quality than them. He might be poor and persecuted, but he was proud and legal. Making his way through this world had been a struggle, and things had not changed. Having a convicted criminal for a son was something that would quite possibly destroy him.

Probably Gillian would wonder where he was. He had a date with her that night, and she might wonder what had happened to him. She would not contact the family. It was not a relationship that his father would have allowed, and he certainly would never allow visitors to the house, especially women. The only individual who was not a family member that had visited the house had been the Probation Officer. That was only because the law required it. He resented it, but was powerless to change it. His house was his private fiefdom, and his family were his peasant slaves whose function in life was to do his will. No, Gillian would not contact the family, but she might send a letter. Was there such a thing as prison-post? He didn't know. He knew so little about prison life. What were all those voices out on the landing? Why did the guard open everyone's door but his? What would happen next? What was expected of him – was he expected simply to sit in his cell quietly and wait for someone to do something? He had never been in this position before. Normally, a person decides what to do and does it. But in a cell with a locked and bolted door, what is there to do? Sit and wait? A guard slid an eyeball across the peephole. The prisoner looked directly at the peephole and offered a thin smile. He could not see if the guard was smiling back. The cover swung back and he heard the jingling of keys. He quickly hid his damaged hand behind his back and smiled as he opened the door. Was this to be another beating?

'Here's yer grub. And keep yer noise down.'

Then he was gone. The door had been open about ten seconds. However, the ten-second gust of freedom made all the difference to the cell. He looked at the food, and then at the door. He would rather have the door left open than the grub. He grabbed the tin strip that served as a knife and poked at the mess on the plate. After he had eaten he needed to use the stinking pot. His hand was smarting badly, and he cuddled it in the handkerchief. For many long hours he then sat staring at the wall, conjuring up imaginary scenarios and people and images in his head and projecting them on to the brick. Later, the guard and his Trustee came along with a large mug of cocoa, scooped from the bucket. Grit-filled, it was rumoured that the cocoa was laced with bromide to discourage erections. The skinny prisoner drank a sip and poured the rest in the pot. \it really was that horrible. Later, after a spell at the window, he got into bed and went to sleep.

Study

Colossians 1:19-23. You are free from accusation because of what Jesus accomplished on the cross. Your sins are forgiven and you have been made holy. Are you living your life as a forgiven person? Are you living your life as a holy person?

Pray

For young people who are coming into the prison system for the first time today. Ask God to give them hope for the future, a sense of being forgiven and true repentance for what they have done wrong. Though they are in prison, ask God to make them truly free.

UNHAPPY PEOPLE

Nine o'clock in the morning was mail time. For a few minutes there would be smiles and bright faces, clean jokes, and genuine happiness. There had always been two emotional experiences at mail time. Prisoners who had been accepted by their loved ones in spite of their crimes would be happy for a while. And those who had been rejected and scorned, who had long ago been driven to hate the world and all it stood for, who had become cynical and emotionally empty, having lost any feelings of love or loyalty. There were not a few of them. Prisoners who suffered in this way would complain quietly or shut themselves in their cells for an hour. Once the happy ones had cooled off a bit, the unhappy ones would engage malicious arguments and suggestions designed to limit their joy. Their mission was to destroy whatever they could, and they often did.

'Well, well, Johnny boy. Got a letter then?'

'Yeah.' Almost apologetically.

'Give us a look, then.'

' No. It's all right. It's only from a girlfriend. You don't want to read my rubbish.'

'Aw, come on. Let's have a quick look.'

'No!'

'Hey, Strangler. Come over here. Johnny-boy's got a sexy letter.'

'Oh, now, don't mate. It's private.'

Strangler and a couple of mates saunter over.

'Look it's private. A private letter. It's not for everyone to read. Why don't you get someone to write to you, then you'll have your own letters to read.'

The unhappy ones throw their arms around Johnny in mock comradeship. One of them makes a grab for the letter, and tears it in half. Johnny by this time has tears of anger in his eyes. Strangler grabs the other half of the letter and begins to read it out in a cartoon voice while his mates hold Johnny down.

He wriggles to get free, but not too much, not wanting to provoke Strangler to some serious reaction. A tear wells up in his eye, and his face goes a deep pink. Half embarrassed, half maddened, he is humiliated and angry. All he can do is repress it inside. He'll get it out of himself later by pummelling the pillow or the wall.

The unhappy ones let him go. Strangler rams the two halves in to Johnny's top pocket. By now, Johnny begins to resent the letter and the girlfriend who sent it. It brought him such shame. The unhappy ones walk away and Johnny's left smoothing the crumpled paper, all alone. Unhappy. The unhappy ones have finished what they set out to do. They didn't realise this about themselves, of course. Such awareness would imply that they had a desire and capacity for reflection. They did not. All they knew was that whenever their antennae detected joy, their job was to squash it and put it out. They did it by instinct. An instinct that had been born and cultured in families that treated children as pieces of flesh, and not as vulnerable elements of impressionable, trusting soul. They were victims as much as their own victims were. To make everyone else like them was their mission. Not by choice, but by destiny.

Men who had letters from girlfriends were envied throughout the prison system. They were envied because they had managed to maintain a spiritual connection with home. They had something they could touch and hold in their hands. Most had not. All most prisoners had were fantasies and other peoples' memories, other peoples' letters. Dreams and perversions. Dissatisfaction. Emptiness. Now and again people had a laugh, but it wasn't a real laugh; it was a mocking, cynical laugh:

> The owl and the pussycat went to sea
> In a beautiful pea-green boat.
> They took some honey,
> And plenty of money,
> Wrapped up in a five-pound note…
> *Wham! Splat! Moan! Crunch! Did 'em over!*
> *Yeah!*

And everyone would laugh at the thought of the Pussycat and the Owl getting mugged for their honey and money. It was sick. It was insane. It was grown-up children acting out their reaction against the abuse they had suffered themselves as children. Their nursery rhymes, instead of being realms of fun and childish fantasy in which violence was sanitised, had become arenas of actual violence and real revenge.

They laughed at the man who had a letter from his girlfriend telling him they were through. They laughed because they were deeply wounded, and the only comfort and ease was to pass it off as a joke. These were unhappy people who lived in an unhappy world.

Then one day the skinny prisoner woke in the morning with an idea. 'Why not capitalise on it?' Before the day had passed, he had thought of a way of gaining some respect from the other prisoners. Write some stories for the unhappy prisoners. What they lacked in prison was sex, so write some sexy stories. It would earn some tobacco on the one hand and provide them with some entertainment on the other. What could be wrong about that? It couldn't do any harm.

Later that day he went to the office, where he had been made Cleaner, and 'borrowed' an exercise book. He had also joined an 'English Writing' class, and so had access to pencils, pens and ink. He did pottery, too. Not that that had anything to do with making money from the other prisoners, but it showed that he was interested in learning stuff.

What he eventually began top produce was pretty sexy. It was cool, too. What he lacked in a actual experience, he read in other books, and the rest he made up in his head. During the following weeks he constructed a passable work of art, containing an actual picture of a naked female he had found in one of the bins in the Officers' Club. Unlike today, when the walls of prisoners' cells are plastered with pictures of this kind, in those days it was unheard of to find a single one. It must have been good, because not only the prisoners but also some of the guards made bookings to get their hands on it. One day, he booked it out for two cigarettes and it didn't come back. East come, easy go. But it had the effect the skinny prisoner wanted it to have. It established him as an OK guy, and his life from then on, in that prison at least, was considerably easier than it had been. He was never attacked. Not by any prisoner at least, and he was never raped by anyone. Those two things, he was grateful he escaped throughout his journey as one of the customers, through the prisons of England.

Fantasy stories were not the worst thing that ever happened to prisoners. The worst was probably getting letters from people on the outside. Prisoners, he thought, would do a lot better if there were no such interference from outside. Much better and easier, to just let prison life and its routines of violence, stink, and low-life humour seep slowly into the individual prisoner's psyche over a period of time. Let him just sink as low as it goes, without overblown hopes of a better life or rehabilitation. Let the time merge into a grey mass of goo, un-punctuated by letters and days and dates and clocks. Prisoners could do without all the reminders the mail can bring. Some prisoners especially. One young prisoner on the Second Gantry used to cry himself to sleep every night for a week after getting a letter from home. His wife would write about the things they used to do – places they visited and friend they once had when he had been a free man. She'd write about all this stuff in the hope of reforming him. She had become a Christian during his time in prison, and she thought this kind of thing would encourage him and give him hope. All it did was to drive him to greater despair, until one day we heard he had hanged himself in his cell. He had a picture of a crucifix in his fist.

Another man, in another prison some time later had a similar experience. His wife tried to reform him, and each letter made him increasingly bitter. Each letter tore a bit out of his heart. In the end all he could do was to resent her intrusion into his suffering. He would spend the nights regretting he ever met her. He passed her letters around the prison in a vain attempt to let others into the private world they had created together, and of which she was now reminding him. It was a life he could no longer have. He was emptied by this experience, and never recovered from it. They came and took him away screaming one night after association had ended. He never returned.

But who was to say he was different from any of the rest of them? If anyone else had been through what he had been through and interpreted and felt the experience just as he had done, would they have done any differently?

At that time, the skinny prisoner believed this lad was simply the product of his life experience. He thought that anyone who had been through that experience would react in the same way, whoever and whatever he or she was. At this time he did not know that a person's mind and whole life could be radically transformed by Christ, whatever his or her experience, upbringing, hormones, state of health or genes.

Study

Colossians 2:13-15. Your sins were nailed to the cross with Jesus. All the accusations against you died with Him. Jesus beat the demonic powers at the cross. What does this mean? How can you know His freedom more in your life?

Pray

Prisons have Education facilities and a chapel. Pray for prisoners who are illiterate to learn to read. Pray for prison educators to be encouraged and committed. Pray for the Holy Spirit to infuse prison communities banishing all sources of evil within them, and encouraging all prison chaplains.

'DEAR JOHN'

There was another kind of mail, known in prison circles as a 'Dear John'. This was the letter every prisoner knew would come sooner or later. It was the letter that ought to have been perfumed, from the writing on the envelope, but which was strangely and unexpectedly un-perfumed. It was the letter no-one wanted to open, and which the guard's mail trustee was reluctant to deliver. It smelled official; it carried bad news. It is the letter prisoners take from the Trustee and shut the cell door. You want peace and quiet. You know this letter is designed to help you not too cry too much, but which will make you weep. These were tears that were destined to be cried, right from the first time you met her. You knew there was no escape. Even if you tore the letter to shreds without bothering to read it, still you would know every word, and what those words were saying. How many ways are there, after all, to say what had to be said?

The handwriting was small and round. Feminine, perhaps. He pictured the plump little fingers holding the ballpoint pen, and saw the scrubbed little hands shaking as the words hesitantly came. A little blue smudge marked the spot where distilled sadness had fallen on the paper and made the ink run. He, too, was sad.

'Dearest darling Roy,

Mum and dad saw the paper last night. They said they knew all along you would end up in prison, but didn't want to tell me. They said I wouldn't believe them. I would think their were trying to split us up. They were so cruel. But I know they couldn't help it.

They said I couldn't see you again. They said by the time you get out I would have forgotten you, and in my heart I know they are right. I was getting ready to meet you when the paper came through the door. Why didn't you tell me? I thought we trusted one another...'

Why did she have to write? Couldn't she just simply have forgotten about it all and stayed away, pretending that he never existed? His throat hurt;

the pain in his chest made his eyes run. He wasn't crying...

'...I went to the cinema anyway. Mum said it was the best thing to do. Enjoy myself and try to forget it for a while. Try and forget it! How could I, after all that we have been through? But I knew they were right. They were trying to be kind really. They said it was a phase we were going through, and it would all be right in the end. Let time be a healer, they said. I know they were trying to help, but I feel so alone as I write this. I didn't know what was happening. You sometimes didn't turn up for dates anyway. I kept trying to pretend you had just forgotten again. But it hasn't worked. Sorry to go on. I know you must be pretty upset yourself. It was wonderful while it lasted. Goodbye.'

Goodbye? So sudden? He looked for more words. It had looked pretty good halfway through the letter, and at the end just this. Goodbye! He looked on the reverse of the paper. There were no more words. That was it. All there was, was the straight line of darkened fold across the centre of the page and the marks of the ballpoint pen pressed

through from the other side. Three kisses. Nothing.
He pressed his lips against each small 'x', and
whispered to each, 'Goodbye'.

At last he had become a fully-fledged member of
the prison community. The cutting of this final cord
had absolved him from any responsibility to people in
the outside world. He felt that his destiny had been
fulfilled. He felt the sudden euphoria of having no
responsibilities, no ties, and no reasons to be at any
place or in any time than here and now. From now on
his friends, he decided, would be chosen from among
people who would only be acquaintances. He would
choose from among people who had no identity because
they were all the same, all cut off from people they at
one time loved. They would be people who had no
future because they had no hope. They would be people
who had learned the hard way how fragile and
ephemeral relationships were. A girl had said she loved
him. He had lived in that belief for some months, and
had come to trust it. But with the first gust of wind, the
first bit of difficulty, everything changed. It all fell
away and melted into nothing. He decided then,
somewhat immaturely – but he was only seventeen –
that he would never fall in love again. From now on, it

would be a case of using people rather than being used by them. It hurt too much.

He brushed the books off the scrubbed wooden table. He laid the precious letter down and looked at it. Paper. With words on it. They could have been any words. An address and a stamp licked by her tongue. He stood at the other end of the cell, five paces away from the opened letter. Devastating letter! He waited for the pain in his throat to release the flood of water. It wouldn't go, and he waited patiently. The letter began to fade and to become confused visually with the grain of the wooden table. He re-focussed his eyes, but his vision clouded again just as quickly. He had forgotten the walls and the door and the foul chamber pot. All that existed was the table and the letter and the throbbing pain. He yearned and begged silently for tears to come, because he had read that letting it all out would help. When they finally came, they hurt. Grief always hurts. This was no different except that it threatened to smother him. He had to grieve; after all, it had meant something, after all. Say it as often as he may, it would not make it true that he could stand alone like superman without being touched. It seems that there was a promise to keep. She had cried. Now, he cried. So the tears ran down his nose and ebbed and flowed with his thoughts and emotions. When he thought of the tragedy of it all, the tears flowed, and as each little bit of the tragedy lost its pain, they ebbed. He went through each moment he could remember, each place they had been together, each tenderness they had shared and each touch they had given one another. Ass he wept over each thing, so each thing was healed and cleansed. He wept because he knew it would ease the sorrow. It would end the pain. He did not feel guilty at ending the pain, and by the early morning the following day, all pain had been removed. There was no guilt. He had wanted it to end, and now it had ended. He had enough tragedy surround him as it was. He did not need more. So finally, when each thing had been removed with tears, he was empty. Nothing remained. He read the letter again. It meant nothing any more, and he tore it to pieces without regret or anger and set a match to it. A funeral pyre. He used a whole match as a celebration and as an act of generosity and thanks for something good but done. The ordeal had been suffered and survived.

He stood five paces from the heap of ashes on the table and gazed at it. He had brushed the books off the table and they lay scattered on the floor. The love was now a pile of dust. It had been experienced and enjoyed, but now was gone. A heap of dust piled in a room out of the way of the winds of chance. The little mound of ashes contained the memory of his life. It was his life, and if all he was, was a heap of dust, then everyone was dust. If everyone was dust, what did it matter that some of it was piled away in a prison and other was piled away in a palace. Dust in a prison was undisturbed, but in a palace the wind is blowing and the dust is scattered to the elements. If anything, his was better. His was at peace and resting, not blowing about in the wind. A cell is a hiding-place, a place where a man can hide away and not be worried all day long. The only wind that can disturb you is the kind of event that had happened to him this morning. There was no more wind to be expected. No more could he be disturbed. He had experienced the final gust.

He got down on his knees with the whole spent match in his hand and began picking the muck out from between the floorboards. The match dug deeply into the filthy grease. He lay forward on his stomach, flat on the floor. Stretching out his arms in a crucifix, he fantasised about what it was like to die for someone; to be crucified on the altar of love. The wind howled across the wilderness beyond the prison walls creating a gentle breeze from the open window-grate.

When he cried this time, it was of a different order. He had never wept this way before. It was no longer the weeping of a sad teenaged lover. It was the hollow, shadow land, lonely, echoing howl, which is as silent as the beating of an owl's wing. The sharp, beating pain of a dagger being twisted within the body, where no-one else could see. It was not the weeping of a youth any more. It was the crying of a man who had at last surrendered to the pity of life, the emptiness of despair. Everyone was dust. The girl was forgotten, but the whole world was remembered. And if anything was the subject for despair it was the world itself. If there was a bottomless love somewhere in the universe, he didn't know where or in whom it was to be found.

The sound of the keys and chain of an approaching guard interrupted his self-pitying orgy, and the door opened. The guard was opening all the doors on the landing and did not enter the cell, or even notice that the prisoner in Number 23 was lying prone on the floor. It was time for work. For him, the day did not exist. It dragged on forever, or it flew past in a second. Whatever it was, he could not say. Time had lost its meaning. Something profound had been understood, and it filled his mind. Then the night came and the shouts and bangings and cursings and singing, and the plaintive sound of a mouth organ died down until all was silent. Quiet closed down on the prison where the skinny prisoner lived. Gays shouted their 'Goodnight Love's' until nothing stirred. A man walked his dog on the country path and the wilderness closed around the building.

Study

2 Corinthians 5:14; Titus 3:4-7. God's mercy, kindness and love have made you a new creation. If you know Jesus, you are a different person to who you used to be. What changes have you seen in your life since you met Jesus? What further changes are you hoping for? Thank Him for what He's doing in you.

Pray

Pray for all those who are forced by choice or circumstance to say goodbye. Pray that empty and hopeless captives' lives may be filled with God's love and inspired by His Spirit to become a new creation, and a fertile land for good works.

SEX AND POWER

Borstal boys, young prisoners, and wayfarers who came in for the winter, smoked Black Shag tobacco. Though very rough on the throat it was half the price of regular tobacco. None of these were real convicts, though. They were temporary visitors in a system that was better designed to deal with long-term prisoners. These were people who had been in and out of prison for most of their lives, and expected to spend the rest of their lives doing the same. Some of them reckoned on spending two years living the good life on the proceeds of crime, then being imprisoned for two years in payment for their crimes, and thus it would go on for ever. They never grumbled, but took the whole thing philosophically. They made their cells comfortable, developed a sense of wry humour, got on well with their neighbours, and settled in for the duration. Some of them hung curtains in their rooms, and had regular infusions of marmalade, sugar and tea.

People outside prison sometimes called these kinds of prisoners 'old lags', although there were far more young 'lags' than old ones. These men smoked a more refined brand of tobacco, not Black Shag. Since they were in for the long haul, they had to look after themselves. They had systems organised with the outside world. Whilst a short-term prisoner could get away with smoking this muck for two or three years, to do it for ten years would shorten their lives to an unacceptable degree.

These people had been in the prison system one way or another from generations back. Even a superficial skim through the school and social services records in any English city will quickly reveal the names of families who have had dealings with crime and the prison system. The same family names will occur over generations, so that one could predict with reasonable accuracy which offspring from which trailer park or corporation housing estate would be destined for the prison life. It was not to do with morality or ethics or genetic destiny towards criminality. It was a social and cultural reality. Prison populations were as much, if not more, the result of the accident of birth than of innate or genetic determination. The grandfathers and great grandfathers of these prisoners had been involved in the prison system, as much as the children of these prisoners would be involved also in the system. It was a social fact. This situation would only change if you changed the culture. It was not a problem of morals of a whole English subculture. You couldn't change it by giving these people religion (by which is not meant

'Christian faith', which is a relationship with Jesus Christ and not a religion). The issue of change was not a religious, but a political and relationships one.

The real truth was – and this was a powerful reason why no one ever did anything effective about it – was that criminals were essential for the smooth running of civilised society. The existence of these people was as essential for English social life as was a large pool of unemployed people to run the capitalist system, or sick people to run the health service or posh people to fill the independent schools system. Without people from the criminal subculture, the whole edifice of English civilisation would collapse.

Social determinism was one thing. Morality was another. And these convicts, who were 'old lags', had a morality that was as clear and austere as that of any Puritan divine.

Of an evening the prisoners would watch television in the television room. Because of the fear of riot, these men were locked, with two prison officers, in a large room. The room was four ordinary cells with the dividing walls demolished, and could seat about fifty men, with a television on a high stand at the front. Chairs were arranged in rows, with an aisle down the center, like an evangelical preaching-church, where the congregation's attention was directed towards the pulpit with no distractions.

The pale green light from the screen bathed the group in its flickering luminescence. It was quiz show, and the men were howling their delight at the quizmaster's female assistant. The metal-barred door was locked and the wooden door beyond was closed. One of the guards strolled down the aisle and back again, slapping his nightstick against the crease down his pants. The reality of fifty sexually and socially frustrated prisoners stuffed together into a room with no lavatory and only two guards to keep order did not bear thinking about. The safety ramifications of such a situation were bizarre, should anyone want to make an assessment of it. The prison service was generally understaffed, and this kind of situation, which for this particular prison had become a weekly custom, was fraught with danger. The responsibility of keeping these men in order and pleasant-minded had been devolved to a television presenter who was employed by the BBC and only virtually present in the room.

The skinny prisoner, thinking about these things, was not comfortable in his situation, but had no choice but to accept it. Should one of the prisoners decide to go mad, there would be no way of controlling him. He had visions of the guards being kicked senseless and the men tearing at each other to get out. He dismissed this as the paranoid ramblings of a disturbed mind. He sat back in the canvas chair and settled down to watch the rest of the show. It could not have been more than a few second later – certainly not more than five minutes – that he felt an arm reaching round his shoulders and towards his neck. He shivered. What was happening? He dare not look round, and felt the hand coming closer, until eventually it was laid gently on his shoulder. He froze. What if he leapt up and started to create a fuss? Surely it might be the very thing that started the riot he had been fantasising about. There was nothing he could do. He did not know if this was an accepted part of the prison culture. He looked straight ahead and shifted just his eyes from left to right to see if anyone else had noticed what was happening. No one had. The room was dark and each prisoner was anonymous, and engaged in the programme. The hand began to caress his shoulder and to move down towards his chest. He didn't know what to do. He moved slightly. There was not much room, but there was no way of getting far from the broken teeth and halitosis. He hadn't shaved. His prison shirt collar was frayed. He pitied and feared him...

Suddenly the arm was jerked roughly away. The teeth and smell were wrenched away, and he had gone. There was a silent scuffle and some whispered angry words, then nothing.

Interviewing the leader of a religious community many years later over such an individual's case, the skinny prisoner was told,

'This is a very dangerous individual, who avoids the help that he is offered wherever he goes. He is a controlling personality and does not acknowledge that his behaviour is offensive, even though it is illegal.'

He had a secret password, which he used on all his personal transactions, the logo, 'Melchizedek'. This had a particular significance for someone who thought of himself as a member of the Judeo-Christian faith. The Hebrew = *Malki – sedeq* = 'Sedeq is king'. He was the king of Salem, and a high priest, who blessed Abraham after Abraham had defeated the king of Sodom (Book of Genesis 14:18ff). Note, the name, 'Sodom' and what the word, 'sodomy' refers to. There were at least two significant points in the light of the skinny prisoner's interview with the guardian of the religious community. They were, first, Power, status, and control.

Abraham, the founder of the Hebrew faith, a patriarch of Christianity, and a powerful historical character, submitted to being blessed, in other words, controlled by Melchizedek. This makes Melchizedek more powerful, and of greater *status* than Abraham. Second, it made Melchizedek the King of Sodom. Melchizedek blessed Abraham because he defeated Sodom. In the Hebrew and Christian tradition, this was the world centre of sodomy, considered by both traditions to be a mortal sin.

What did this say about the ephebophile who had attacked the skinny prisoner in the television room all those years ago? It is likely that someone like this who chooses to hide in the Christian community may choose this logo if he felt that it codified the essence of his character and internal emotional processes as a Christian. It would have the added benefit that the word was secret. Only God would know it. It is not remarkable that the long tradition of homophobia in both Hebrew and Christian traditions has set-up powerful emotional conflicts in some Christian homosexuals. Many evangelical Christians hate them. What was remarkable in this instance, however, was that this sex offender chose the name Melchizedek as his logo – a name that produced the essence of his internal conflict. He saw himself as an individual who had such power that he is qualified to bless the Patriarch,

Abraham, the man who defeated Sodom, and, ironically, condemned sodomy, the very act that he was engaged in, being himself a sodomite!

Taking this Old Testament name, Melchizedek, the author of the Book of Hebrews in the New Testament, equated the Old Testament Melchizedek with Jesus Christ Himself. Melchizedek, according to the author of Hebrews, *is* Jesus Christ, the Saviour - Hebrews Ch.5. verses 6 to 11, and 6:20 to 7:28.

For these two reasons, the religious community leader felt that this was a dangerously sick man. It seemed significant to the skinny prisoner that the leader thought he saw himself as the 'Saviour, not just the helper' of vulnerable young men', especially in the light of the fact that before the skinny prisoner told him, he had not known that he had chosen the password, 'Melchizedek' to apply to himself. This provided an important insight into the nature and internal processes of this individual. The technical books about this say that paedophile males who have an exclusively male child preference have twice the recidivism-rate of paedophile males who have a female-exclusive condition. Put another way, this ephebophile's condition was twice as resistant to 'cure' as that of someone who preferred female children. This did not mean that the prisoners treated him with kid gloves. In fact, their approach was much more head-on. They didn't take the trouble to 'analyse this', they just cut his testicles off that night after lights out. Who let them in to his cell, no one knew. It had been planned for many weeks previously. It did not happen as a direct result of his attack on the skinny prisoner earlier that evening.

Three days after this event, when he first heard what had happened, the skinny prisoner went to his room and was sick. The convicts had discovered the man's history. Maybe one of the guards had told them, or one of the Trustees in the admin department had rifled through the files. No one knew how they had found out, but they had discovered he was in prison for a sex crime, and had not been put on Rule 43 for his own protection. It was said later that he didn't care about himself, and that when the time had come for him to undergo his torture from the convicts, he was quite glad about it. In a lawless society, there had to be some ways of maintaining the pecking order, even among people who had no respect for other laws. There was an overwhelming hatred against all sex criminals, except, for some strange reason, against rapists. Perhaps it was the thought of perverted sexuality – perhaps it was, as some people said, the thought of some individual actually doing what a lot of men only fantasized about doing. Perhaps it was these convicts' way of punishing themselves in some perverted and repressed way, for the things they knew lay deep in their own souls, but which they were unwilling and unable to acknowledge. As consumers of whatever rubbish was peddled on the television advertisements, and for a lot of these men in the girly magazines off the top shelf, they had little moral strength to stand against it. They knew this about themselves, only secretly, and felt secretly guilty about it. In the end, it really was a way of choosing a scapegoat and sending it off, on its lonely journey, into the wilderness. It was a way of atoning for their guilt. It was a way of making the unrighteous righteous, the hopeless hopeful, and the condemned redeemed. It was a secular way of making a blood sacrifice for the community's sins, and in an ironical twist, the sinner had become the saviour. The scapegoat had been the source of the community's new life. Both prisoners and guards felt cleansed by the paedophiles suffering. The act had been done, and now they could start afresh with a new life.

These things happen in the Nick. A sex crime, if it is not rape, is the worst crime that can be committed. It is the single crime all convict hate. They do not try to understand it, because understanding takes too long, and while you're busy understanding it, it still goes on. The quickest way, they think, is a knife or a boot. After all that was what the system had done to them. The thing about a sex crime in particular is that all the cons are locked away. The wife is at home, and it's a lucky prisoner who can totally trust his wife and be happy about it. He never knows how she is, or how his kids are. If anything drastic did happen to them, would his wife tell him? It's more likely that he wouldn't hear a thing about it. She wouldn't want to upset him, and she would prefer to sort it out without his help. The old lag knows that if anything bad were to happen, his wife would water it down and feed it to him slowly, in drops, so it wouldn't seem so bad. If she did tell him in a letter or on the telephone, the governor wouldn't let it through anyway. The last thing he wanted was a riot on his hands, or yet another suicide. The convict knows all of this. The way to ease his mind was to try and murder or at least seriously injure every sex criminal he could get his hands on. It was am kind of gesture or symbol that even though he was miles away from home and locked up away from his family, and unable to help if trouble came, he was still in his masculine role as defender of the family from sexual marauders and predators.

This had been an example of the kind of help a con will give. It was help. However much the one who is helped in this way may not like it or fell that it is wrong, how can you say to someone who has done this that you are not grateful to have been saved from being raped and buggered in the prison lavatory? There is nothing you can say, and there is nothing else you can be but saved. You are grateful, but degraded and appalled. Nor can you blame yourself, because it is an inevitable process, as ingrained in the prison culture as loving one another is ingrained in the Christian Gospel. All you can do is retreat to your cell and be sick.

How can you thank a man for mangling another man? You can't. You just light up a cigarette, punch the wall, count the bars again, climb up on your chair and gaze wordlessly across the silent heath. You close your eyes and pretend it is not happening, and look forward to the time of your release.

The man was in hospital for three weeks. When he came out, he was placed on Rule 43. That meant that he was to be given protection. That meant that he would be locked in close confinement with the cell door opened only for meals to be delivered and to empty his chamber pot. He had mailbags brought in for him to sew, which he worked on every hour of every working day. Forbidden to mix with the other prisoners, he was condemned to a life of solitude and silence. He had to eat alone, sleep alone, exercise alone and do everything alone. How many times did he count the bricks in the cell walls? If he called from his window, no one answered. If he banged his pot, no one responded. Often, if he rung his alarm bell, the guard would take his time and sometimes not respond at all.

He had no friend or any kind of companionship except his own tortured mind. To be so much alone must wrench the soul out of any man who did not have a monkish vocation. He would end up an empty husk, a discarded chrysalis. He hums a little tune and occasionally talks to himself. He lived for months in that little cell and probably kept a record of every stitch he put into the mailbags during that time.

As this is written, Jesus is being thought about. Is Jesus like that man? Despised, rejected. Even now the thought is too repulsive to bear. His teeth had been kicked out; he had internal injuries; he had been genitally injured and his nose had been broken. For weeks he looked barely human. It was said that a knife had been used, but none of the Trustees reported any unusual police activity in that time. It happened, and it was forgotten. That was all.

Study

1 Peter 2:23-24. We are healed by Christ's death. How has Jesus healed you? Physically? Emotionally? Relationally? Ask Him for more wholeness and healing today. Be as specific as you can.

Pray

Pray for all who work in the prison system – for uncertain employment prospects and difficult working conditions. Pray for the changing of hearts, the transformation of lives, and for all who seek to bring healing. Pray for all victims, and for psychologists and psychiatrists and prison counsellors.

THE MARK OF THE BEAST

Sean and Kraig had been friends for years. They had been through the Approved School system together, and had both served a term of borstal training. Friends on the outside, they came from the same estate, and their friends and families on the outside coincided almost identically. They were cousins.

Kraig was the hard man between them. Sean was his mate. At some time in the distant past Kraig had made an impression on his cousin that, with the occasional reminder in the form of a light beating, had never disappeared. Whereas Sean was more of a thief, Kraig was more of a violent character. His behaviour on the outside was renowned among the police and in his community.

If Kraig was after someone, everyone else stood out of the way. He had a girlfriend, Kelly, who was also known for her violent behaviour and fearlessness of any male or female in her social circle. No lad on the estate would stand against her. This was partly because she was Kraig's woman, and they feared his psychotic behaviour, but also because in her own right she was a very capable and fearless fighter. She was also an alcoholic, and a beaten woman. She was a woman who loved her man too much.

Kraig's possessiveness made her a victim of regular fierce beatings when he was on the outside, and when he was in prison there were a group of people who kept an eye on her to make sure she behaved herself sexually. This was something she was not apt to do, especially when drunk and unable to master her instincts. Frankly, when she had been on the town, she would have sex with anyone without discernment. Her regular contraceptive depot injection effectively prevented any pregnancies. Drinking-and-then-sex was her weakness, and Kraig knew about it. Needless to say in a middle class or liberal or radical feminist culture, she would have the right to do what she wanted with her own body. That she was the personal property of no man – especially since she was not married to him.

However, this was not middle England, and this was not the case for Kelly. Hers was working-class English criminal culture, and she belonged to the man who owned her in the same way that his motorcycle belonged to him, and just as he could buy and sell his motorcycle, he could do what he wanted with her. The single dynamic that held the relationship together was his violent behaviour and her need to be loved violently.

Whereas she had to be sexually exclusive, sleeping and living only with Kraig, he was permitted to do as he liked. This was the way things were meant to be. There was an implicit agreement in the relationship that she could complain if he were unfaithful, and could hit him freely without retribution. But in the end, he could sleep around and she could not, although she did.

She was unable to leave him, for if she did, she would be badly beaten and could be reasonably killed for her disloyalty. In addition, where else would she find someone to possess and punish her, as she had witnessed her own mother's lifelong punishment from her now absent father? That was the threat. Everyone knew it, and it was real.

These two men joined the skinny prisoner in his single cell, and stayed for the weeks that led up to his transfer to the Allocation Wing of Wormwood Scrubbs.

Sensing their superiority not only in numerical but also in terms of their willingness to be depraved, he acceded to their demand to have the best of the beds. That was, the two beds at floor level. The cell, designed for what the Victorians considered was enough for a single prisoner, had three beds jammed in to it. One set of metal-framed bunk beds, and a single metal bed.

This left a half-metre wide strip of floor space between the three beds. With the small table carrying the water-jug and wash bow, this left room for the communal chamber pot and little else. The cell was cramped and overcrowded. It was a recipe for stress and disaster, especially for the skinny prisoner, being in the company of two violent characters such as Kraig and Sean.

The skinny prisoner quietly took the top bunk-bed and said nothing. Scared out of his wits, he said little during the following weeks. He spent as little time out of the bed as possible, leaving the floor to them. He piled his clothes on the foot of his bed in a neat heap and tied some string around them to keep them from falling to the floor. He concentrated on causing as little disruption to their lives as possible.

They never threatened him directly, though. Nor did they hurt him in any way – or not directly. His fear was fear of the unknown. Not knowing at all who these people were or what they might be capable of. He knew there was a bond between them, and suspected that it was family. Their conversation was always amiable together, and there were rarely any threats, though their talk was a string of basic Anglo-Saxon. They would sit up into the small hours talking and making jokes together, ruminating over their lives and friends and commitments on the outside. Sean often talked about his girlfriend, but Kraig only rarely mentioned Kelly. Most of their talk was about their families on the outside and what they were going to do when they got out. They had plans for starting a club, and there was a possibility of putting their string of part-time sexual contacts and girlfriends on the streets.

Many nights were spent in planning and projecting ideas. If life was about surviving in the prison system, these two young men had got it all worked out. It was, of course, fantasy.

It was Tuesday night, and the skinny prisoner had been quiet all evening as usual. He was reading a comic book in the top bunk. Sean was quietly finishing-off a tattoo on his arm. It was a matchstick figure of The Saint. The skinny prisoner winced every time the poisoned needle jabbed into Sean's naked flesh. He just sat there, stopping now and again to admire the work as he did it. Occasionally he wiped away the blood. The needle jabbed deftly into the black lead polish cradled in his groin, then into his arm; time and again. His face was impassive and concentrated, like the face of a shaman on another planet. Not a sound came from his lips. Not even his breathing showed signs of pain. It might not have been his own arm at all for all the concern and involvement he had shown. Jab-jab-jab-wipe; jab-jab-jab-wipe; jab-jab-jab-wipe. He finished, wiped the mess from his arm, and admired the completed job. Even before the blood had stopped flowing he rolled his sleeve down and began packing the grate polish and needle away in their rags.

In prison tradition, the tattooing needle was made by breaking off the end of a plastic toothbrush, sticking a needle in the table and heating the eye-end to red-hot. The broken stump of toothbrush was then pressed against the hot needle eye until it had sunken in to the plastic to about half an inch. It was then left to cool and harden. The result was a plastic handle with a needle protruding from it. This could be used as a 'jabber' very effectively.

He hummed gently to himself and beat out a rhythm with his shoulders.

'Hey, Kraig?' He said.

'Hello,' said Kraig from under his blanket.

'What do yet think about giving our old mate Roy here a tattoo?'

Roy had not been consulted about this. He did not desire to bear the mark of the beast Sean for the rest of his life.

'Hmmm,' said Kraig. He wasn't really bothered.

The skinny prisoner sighed with relief and turned over in his bunk to demonstrate that he was asleep anyway.

'Hey Roy, come down here a minute.'

The knell had sounded. He got out of his bed and climbed to the floor where Sean was waiting to puncture him.

'You've got to have a tattoo. Everybody's got at least one.' Said Kraig. It seemed he *was* bothered after all. He sat obediently on the edge of the bed and made a good display of really wanting such a tattoo. He grinned widely and agreed to the abusive operation. People like Sean have no higher intuition or empathy that might inform them that the other person, though expressing agreement is actually reserving what they are truly feeling. It was, in that sense, something Roy brought upon himself because of his cowardliness in failing to say 'no'. He knew this, and despised himself for it.

'What do yer want?' Inquired Sean

He thought quickly. That ' Saint' tattoo was a bit too much and would cause too much pain, and would take nights of prolonged agony to get right. Sean had been working on his for over a week. Not that one, then. He thanked his parents for giving him a short Christian name, and said,

'Do my name. I always did want to see my name in print.'

'Eh?' Sean was a little surprised. He though that at least a 'Saint' would be wanted.

'Well, you see, I've never had a tattoo before, so I'd best be careful first time. Have a small one first, and then maybe something bigger later. If it takes, like. I mean, I might be allergic to black lead, maybe. What do you think?'

Visiting the dentist has nothing on getting a manually applied prison tattoo visited upon you by a working class criminal shaman lacking a conscience. The pain was not something he accept, because acceptance implies choice, and he had no choice. It was something he endured. It had very little to do with him, in fact. It had much more to do with the tattooist's pleasure than the victim's pain. It was more an act of violence, abuse, and intrusion, of violation, than of beautifying the skin. It had more to do with power than love and with ugliness than beauty. In these respects it was like a rape, and taking place against the victim's will but with his oral consent, then it was a complex rape that would carry guilt and shame for evermore.

This skinny prisoner was angry and impotent, yet having to accede and smile. It was a repetition of his relationship with his human father.

The infernal needle pierced the flesh over and over again, carving out a tract of flesh and filling it with poison for over three hours. The first piercing was not deep enough.

'Mmmm, that's no good. We'll have to go deeper if it's going to take properly.'

So in it went, deeper this time, like a dog's dull teeth bruising and tearing at the living flesh. It truly was torture, for there was no other way to describe it; no other category into which this experience fitted. It was an unwilling experience on every level of human consciousness, and it offended every one of the senses, including, most painfully, the moral one.

He clenched his teeth. and then his fist, in the hope of avoiding the next jabbing intrusion. All the time he was thinking that this violation would be with him as a constant reminder on his left arm for the rest of his life. It would be his personal reminder of concentration camp tattoos, and the black-and-white grainy-filmed people trudging jerkily to their deaths at the hands of creatures unworthy of the designation, 'human' flashed through his mind. He immediately felt guilty that he had for a second compared his experience with theirs. He thought of that other Jew who offered Himself freely to the torturers, who he had heard about at Sunday school. Was He here today, on this night of the branding?

'Ough!'

'Wassup?' As though nothing was up.

'Nothing. Just singing to myself. How's it going?'

'Well, keep still then.' He punctuated his remark with an especially deep jab that chipped the bone. The skinny prisoner kept his pain to himself from then on.

The whole abusive business had arisen out of boredom. A prisoner had as much time to read books and do as many tattoos as he wanted in prison. In the end all it added up to was one long, great boredom. There were many prisoners who had tattooed themselves; some had covered enormous expanses of their bodies from utter boredom. Most of them regretted it, but as one prisoner, who had tattooed a 'cut along dotted line' motif across his throat and a dark blue spider web on his face said, 'What else is there to do, especially if you can't read or write?'

As an adult later in life he was to reflect that he had done some pretty meaningless things in his life, but none of them were anywhere near as empty and defeating and soul-grindingly boring as being in prison. Day after day with nothing to do and night upon night reading the same books you've already read three times before, and books that you are not even interested in. All the time you would be thinking of the day of release. Not that the day of release held anything except the end of imprisonment – not great riches or an interesting job or even a family to go to.

The day the gate would open would be the day you would be facing an empty street alone. Was it something to look forward to? Probably not, put like that. Prison behind. Future in front empty.

You would dream and fantasize about the things you would do on release. You would find a woman and have long and often tantric sex. Every freedom-thought was connected in some way with bodily functions - sex, food, walking in the sunshine, swimming, having a holiday and getting a tan. The whole reason for being alive was to get out of confinement and into freedom.

One day the guard came to the cell door. His keys could be heard jingling as usual. He opened the door and ordered the skinny prisoner out. It was time for him to re-appear at another hearing in court at a village called Kings Lynn, deep in rural Suffolk. He was informed that he had to attend another hearing, this time for larceny and housebreaking.

He went with the guard to the courthouse. He went through the hearing. He got his sentence. He returned to prison and was locked up again. All in the course of a day. It meant nothing to him. He deliberately did not drink in the countryside as they sped to their destiny, nor did he notice it on the return journey. He did not want his heart broken by the reminders of sight and smell and hearing of what freedom really meant. The smell of grass; the sound of the railway engine, the sight of people walking freely through the little village of Kings Lynn. These things mocked him. They did not cheer or encourage him. They depressed his spirit rather than caused it to soar. He neither noticed not enjoyed the sounds and sights and smells of freedom. If anything, they served only to make him more hateful, more resentful, more persecuted.

All those people in the court had come to see him punished. They got a buzz out of it. They received their 'justice'. No doubt some of them had been his victims. He had broken in to their homes and stolen their property. They deserved to see him punished. Country people had been known to kill burglars in the past. He had perhaps been lucky in their opinion. Most of the people thronging the public gallery had nothing to do with it. They were bored, lonely people looking for entertainment in the thrill of the courts, and a group of sixth formers doing 'civic studies' observing the local judicial system in operation. It was an irony that the prisoner criminal felt morally disgusted by the respectable people who had come to see him condemned. In his own view he was an abused child, but his thinking was way before his time. It would take ten years for psychologists and social theorists to catch up, and thirty for child protection legislation to follow.

He stood in the dock. Eighty pounds in his socks. They weighed not him but the evidence and judged him. He pleaded guilty anyway, so there was no debate. It hurried the proceedings, and there had been no point in denying it. Had it delivered him back into prison any earlier he would have pleaded double-guilty.

Back in the cell Sean and Kraig took up where they had left off on his tattoo. It was going to say, '*ROY*' when it was finished. He had begun to wonder who the hell 'Roy' was. The whole idea had sounded stupid in the beginning. He knew very well who Roy was. It was him. It was he, himself, the person who lived in his own body. Roy Catchpole. *He* was Roy.

But the question had persisted. It hadn't been drummed into him as much as it had been *needled* into him.

While the tattoo was being finished off during the remaining few days, he argued with himself about who he was. He compared himself in relation to his history, his family, his friends, his home community, his school, teachers, and the people who lived on his street and in his estate. He compared himself beside his relatives at home and his friends in the coffee bars in town. He went through the places where he spent his time in town and the things he thought were important. The Dimpey Café in Stowmarket, the Gaumont cinema in Ipswich and the Safe Harbour pub on his estate, where at age eight he used to climb onto the roof for pigeons' eggs and where at sixteen he used to sing of an evening in the bar with the band, a piano and drums and a microphone. He was not a drinker, but he loved singing for its own sake. They moved a jukebox in and the live music went out of the window. It was rubbish anyway.

He thought of the girlfriend he had spent almost every evening with, and of the girl on the trailer park with whom he had had his first sexual experience in a disused American aircraft hangar. Peggy. She had been sent to borstal a few months earlier than he.

He ruminated on the country walks and the horse riding, the river and the fishing as a child with his father, and the day he almost drowned in the weir. Birds chirping in the hedgerows. His father had been an old countryman and knew the names of every tree and bird and animal that ever there was in Suffolk.

Was that all there was, though? He had been earning a reasonable wage for a youngster, and occasionally he would go to the bowling alley. The work had been hard, though. Working with hessian sacks that were used to store grain on the farms. It was heavy work but he enjoyed it. He was young, and although he was skinny, he was strong. It had been hard work, but he enjoyed the activity. All the time the needle had been going in. Jab, jab, jab. Short jabs with the pain in the point. He had winced once or twice but |Kraig had pretended he hadn't noticed.

He tried to get back to thinking about his home and his green fields, of thinking about his house and his job. He thought again about his three brothers and the horses, and the hours watching television like a zombie. He thought of the wasted hours in front of that machine, and how he could have used the time better on something more fulfilling. He could have been a lawyer even...

He stopped himself from thinking at that point. He chose instead to withstand the pain of the needle. He decided it hurt less than the pain of remorse and resentment. There was nothing he could do about what had gone. It was all in the past. He reflected that he was a criminal, and like a leopard, he could not change his spots. In deciding then and there to live each day as it came, he had put down a marker against the past. There was after all no one to blame but himself. Accept the inevitable and come to terms with what is real. Do not look for *meaning*. Live for today and enjoy everything *now*. Sweet relief came when Kraig stopped jabbing on the fourth day.

'All done.' He announced cheerfully.

'You didn't half make a fuss at first,' he said disarmingly.

'Yeah. S'pose so,' he replied. Don't know why I made such a fuss after all. Maybe because I wasn't used to it. Anyway, it didn't hurt half as much as I thought it would. Bit of a doddle, really. I'll have another one sometime.'

'Yeah. You do that. You'll get a scab on that in a few days time. That's how you'll know it's really working. When you get a scab that's how you know you've got a good tattoo. Watch the screws, though. If they see it, you'll get banged up, down the block in chokey.'

'The block' is the familiar diminutive for the punishment block. 'Chokey' is a form of prison punishment. It consists mainly of being locked away in solitary confinement in the 'block' without association. There are refinements to this punishment however, such as a bread-and-water diet, deprivation of cigarettes and association, and the withdrawal of human company including working with others. Any work is brought to the chokey-cell. The maximum time for chokey with the bread-and-water diet refinement is three days. So although the visiting magistrate or governor may want to give a prisoner more than three days, it has to be suffered three days on and three days off, so that each period of starvation is interspersed with an equal amount of time on a normal diet. For example if a prisoner is given fifteen days bread-and-water, it has to take twenty-seven days to complete at the minimum. A sentence of fifteen days chokey, or being sent 'down the block' can eat up almost a whole month of a prisoner's time, and often this is not counted towards his sentence, so it is time totally wasted. In the block, there is no point in ticking off the days from your sentence, because strictly speaking they don't exist. They are outside of time. They are extra to your sentence. They are also a sentence that can be imposed without due process. They are, strictly speaking, outside the legal system also, and a means of imprisoning an individual without the consent of a jury.

The tattoo could easily attract such a sentence. And who is going to admit that the tattoo was tantamount to a rape? Many are the prisoners who have been raped in this way by their peers and than illegally imprisoned by their captors for having been thus raped.

Study

Galatians 6:4 Paul had a lot to boast about in human terms, but the only thing he is proud of is what God has done in his life. The world has no hold on him – is this true of you? What is more important to you than Jesus?

Pray

Jesus was innocent of any crime, but He transformed His apparent victimhood into triumph. Pray for all victims of violence, whether they are victims of socially unacceptable illnesses, such as alcoholism or AIDS, or of other peoples' wrongdoing. Pray for all beaten men and women, and for their abusers. Pray for all whose need is to be victimised.

OTHER WORLDS

The day came for transfer to Wormwood Scrubbs. It had not come a day too soon. The skinny prisoner had been given a cell of his own for the past week, and was no longer under the constraints of his two enforced compatriots.

Stories abounded about the Scrubbs, as you would expect. The prison itself was a place that housed some of the country's most difficult prisoners. On the other hand, it was also the location of a borstal allocation facility. These were lads of all sorts and conditions, from vulnerable teenagers who were mentally ill more than criminal, to criminal characters who had come through the system and were destined by both culture and choice to a life of crime.

Wormwood Scrubbs was supposed to be a 'hard' prison, in which there was little compassion and no room for error. Breaking the rules would be punished and no quarter given. All of this remained to be seen. Meanwhile the prisoner in his exclusive cell looked forward with anticipation to his move up the system towards his eventual freedom.

He looked at his new tattoo, the new status symbol that marked him out as a criminal of a particular social class and ethnic culture. Let everyone see it. Wear it as a badge of pride. Be silent but strong. Frankly, he was scared witless that he was going to Wormwood Scrubbs, and he did not know how he would cope.

Alone after all this time, he had forgotten what it was to reflect and think clearly and to pace the room in contemplation and silent debate. He had lost the knack. But something had to be done to psyche him up for the impending and inevitable move. He did not know, and there was no way of finding out, what the future had in store for him. He did not know if there were single cells at the Scrubbs, or what the guards were like, or what the daily routine might be. Did the prisoners work, or were they locked up in the cells most of the day? Was there a period of association in the evenings, and were the young prisoners like him thrown in with the older men?

With the impending move and reallocation all books had been removed from the cell, except for the

Bible. It had become an old but un-consulted friend over the months. Always there, but never turned to. He had never made any attempt to read it. He felt that he couldn't, for some reason. Not that he had any idea what was in it. He was just never interested in that sort of thing. They always leave a Bible in your cell. Makes you feel guilty – sorry for your sins. What the prisoners did was, when they told a lie, crossed their fingers and crossed their keys and swore on their mother's life, or their brother's life or some life that was not their own! That way, you could do what you liked but not be guilty. Funny thing, superstition. But when there is a lack of education, that's what you get. These were the kind of people the skinny prisoner had to live with. It was just as well to understand where they were coming from.

He looked around his cell. The high window, the wooden table, the steel-framed bed and noisy horsehair-filled mattress. The Bible. It was a funny thing, but the skinny prisoner had inherited a respect for the Bible. It said, 'Holy' on the cover. Maybe it meant 'special' or 'religious'. He didn't know. Nor did he have any idea if anyone believed in it. Perhaps there were millions. Maybe there were none. He smiled at the thought of all those people swearing on it in court. Most of *them* he knew, didn't believe in it, and hadn't ever read it, so how could they? He had sworn on it himself, and had no idea what was between its covers. No one on the bench had challenged him, and his solicitor had not even mentioned it to him. A Bible was something people had around the house, around prisons and hotels, and used as a magic charm in criminal courts. It was like crossing your fingers and your keys before you told a lie to avoid the punishment for lying, or to make the liar safe. It was superstition, a talisman, and a sacred cow.

He got in to bed, rattled around his horsehair-filled pillow and eventually dropped off to sleep.

He woke again at eleven o'clock and lay there feeling fearful and oppressed. There were butterflies in his stomach and his heart palpitated irregularly. His thoughts only added to his fears. He thought of the time, just over a week ago, when he had been crammed into his cell with two others, Sean and Kraig. Kraig was a Satanist. His talk was of witchcraft and demon possession, and his expectations of life were entirely negative. He hated people, he trusted no-one, pain, he did not feel, family held no mystery or value for him. What mattered was not even money. What really counted was power. Power was all. He used to say that the good thing about power was, whilst power corrupted, absolute power corrupted absolutely. To prove his point he was able to point to public figures that had been good in lower profile jobs, but became transformed into bad people when they had been given bigger jobs and greater powers.

He had 'dark' powers, he claimed. These were powers that he was able to exercise through the recitation of certain charms and the performance of certain rituals. He had learned these arts, he claimed, from his ancestors.

One night, at about this time, half past eleven, he had asked him if he believed in Satan. Since Kraig obviously believed in it, the skinny prisoner decided it was politic to agree. He did not think it would be wise to challenge Kraig's faith, having none of his own. Nor did he want him to get back onto the subject of tattoos again. He felt he would rather humour the Satanist than suffer torture again at his hands.

'Well, depends what you mean, Kraig. If you are saying there's evil about, there's plenty of it out there – and in here, I reckon.'

'What I mean is, do you believe there's a person called Satan?'

'Well, put it this way, do you believe in it?'

All he had hoped to do was keep the conversation going and divert him from thinking about tattoos again.

He had not expected the conversation to take the turn it was about to do.

'Do you want to see his face?

'Eh? Whose?'

'Satan's!'

By this time the skinny prisoner was frightened for a different reason than the tattoo. He was not personally religious, nor really superstitious, although sometimes he would be careful not to step in the cracks in the sidewalk, or walk under a ladder, but that was like obsessive-compulsive disorder, not religion. He had heard about witches and spells and devil-worship and of satanic abuse. Although no one really believed in it, it was frightening nevertheless.

'Get your clothes off and put a sheet around you!' He ordered. 'Sit in this circle.' He had drawn an open circle on the floor. After making some rough drawings and symbols around the circle, before he closed it, he ordered the skinny prisoner to step into it. He did as he was told. Anything to stop an argument and avoid another week of violent jabbing. Then Kraig closed the circle with his victim inside it. Kraig then launched into a series of chants and mumbo-jumbo that could have been anything from precognitive ramblings to satanic tongues. The skinny prisoner had no way of telling. He just wanted to be left unabused. He was not looking for a new faith, or any new introductions.

'Right. Say the Lord's Prayer backwards!'

After many mistakes and repeats, the victim finally managed to get to the beginning of the Prayer starting at the end more-or-less accurately, having been prompted by the Satanist line-by-line. No reason was given for this strange practice, and none was requested. However, by this time the prisoner was pretty scared. Thinking at the beginning that this was just a harmless prank, a way of passing the time, and of evading another tattoo, he had begun to wonder if it were not more serious than he had at first imagined. Psychologically trapped by fear of the mad and conscience-less Kraig, and of the unknown, and physically constrained in a two-by-three metre cell containing three beds and three adult humans, he was unable to remove himself from the satanic circle.

Suddenly, out of the mouth of Kraig came a loud curse. It must have been heard halfway down the gantry. Even Sean, who had been quietly concentrating on picking his feet looked up. He didn't comment. He looked up with a stupid vacant expression with his mouth open and stared. Had Satan actually appeared at the window, neither Kraig nor Sean nor the Skinny prisoner would have been surprised.

Then Kraig said,

'If you want to see Satan's face, you'll have to give him your soul.'

Give him my soul? He could not speak, let alone hand over his soul. What was his 'soul' anyway? And why would anyone want it, whatever it was? He did not know at that time that the idea of a 'soul' separate from the body, as some sort of entity floating around independently on his physical life was a Greek philosophical idea. It was nothing to do with Christian faith.

The Christian idea of 'soul' comes from the Hebrew faith, and that is to do with the physical body. The whole person. This meant that giving your soul to Satan would require you to give every day and every preoccupation and thought to evil deeds, not some airy-fairy idea about giving something metaphysical. He was ignorant, and that was why he was afraid

'Well, yeah, of course. Naturally.' He stammered, more frightened of Sean and Kraig than of anything spiritual.

'Well. Do yer or don't yer?'

'Yeah. Er, I do.'

The cell went quiet. Kraig stopped shouting and moving around in his agitated fashion. The skinny prisoner stood erect and stared at the window grating for a full ten minutes, waiting for something to happen. Would he see the actual face of Satan? Ten minutes and nothing. Well, where was 'it' then? Satan had not appeared to him. He never really thought he would. He shot a glance toward Kraig, expecting him to be laughing. But Kraig's face was deadly serious and pallid. His jaw was strained and taut against the skin. Was it his imagination, or did Kraig's eyes seem deeper set than half an hour ago? The prisoner stepped forward, out of the thrall of the circle. His sheet fell to the floor. Gripping the lapels of his prison windcheater – something he would never have dared to do before for fear of a beating – the skinny prisoner shook him gently, trying to get him to admit he had been fooling.

As he stood there, that night, naked, something told him he had seen something he would not understand for many years to come. Kraig levered the little limpet off and went to bed.

Staring at the barred window for most of that night, wishing something would happen because of the grinding boredom of prison life, the skinny prisoner almost wished that a spectre or phantom would appear and brighten up his life.

Some months later he was to come across a Bible verse in Ephesians chapter six and verse twelve. It started him thinking about all of this again. Originally written in Greek, it carried a harrowing concept. It was about the real spiritual world, not the world imagined in the psychotic fancies of Kraig. It foretold the future role of the skinny prisoner within this spiritual world:

" For we are not struggling against flesh and blood, but against the principalities, against the powers, against the world rulers of this present darkness, against the spiritual hosts of wickedness in the heavenly places. "

Some weeks before, one of the Christians at the Education Centre had given him a book about demons by a Pentecostal Christian, in which there was a picture, presented as true fact, of an exorcism. It said,

'...in the bedroom disgusting spirits anticipated the visit of the Christian minister. They watched the doorway from their positions on the wardrobe, the tops of doors, in every spot, and their breathing sounded like the hauling of shackles through rock-strewn mud... Piercing

screams! Rumbling! Yellow teeth revealed by the lips drawn back to gnaw! The demons sprang from the walls, corners, every alcove of the room and like tiny bleeding and foaming darts went for the Christian's heart...'

Was it fiction? Thinking that it must be fictional, he had gone back to the blurb on the cover and to the foreword of the book, but there it was. It was a serious work by a Christian publisher, purporting to be recording the actual truth of an historical event.

On his last night at that prison, remembering the event with Sean and Kraig in the cell, he experienced that old fear again. He was alone. Dead scared, half expecting the phantoms that had failed to appear when Kraig was there. He got out of bed and laid his hand on the Gideon Bible that lay on the table. He opened it and stuck his finger in at random, looking for something to give him comfort or courage or reassurance. His finger had landed on Ephesians chapter six and verse twelve!

He stuck the Bible under his pillow and had some fitful sleep. He felt it was a stupid thing to do, but it gave him comfort. His thoughts that night were of immense cosmic spiritual battles between good and evil, right and wrong. There were imaginings of monsters and gargoyles straight out of Heironymus Bosch and the Book of Revelation. There were large red crosses flapping in the wind on the flags of crusaders, the bleeding bodies of pagans thrown into ditches, and visions of a Saviour dying on a cross in Palestine many years ago.

He had never thought of religion or mythology before, but it made for an interesting, though sleepless night. The evening with Kraig had obviously created new synapses in an area of his brain that had not been ventured into for a long time. For that much at least he was grateful.

What did the strange coincidence of the bible verse mean? Was it just that? On the other hand, had it been something that pointed beyond? He couldn't say, but brightened up a bit with the thought of tomorrow and being able to see the outside world. It might not be anything special at Wormwood Scrubbs, but at least he would see plenty on the journey there. He got out of his bed at the opening of his cell door for the last time, took up his stinking chamber pot and marched down the gantry to the lavatories, pouring the offensive contents down the communal drain.

This drain was a specially constructed sink that served as an open sewer for all the prisoners. Above the there were two huge cold water taps. Before opening the cells in the morning, the guards would turn these taps full on. They were the first sound prisoners heard every morning. The guards would then open each cell, and the prisoners line up with their pots in hand, slopping the contents down the drain one after the other. The activity is known as 'slopping out', which was exactly what it consisted of. The stink was appalling, and the activity was one that every prisoner, high or low, had to engage in. The smell had worked its way in to every brick in every prison wall. The distinctive smell of English prisons, if they do have a predominant smell, is the stench of stale urine and human excrement.

It is the first thing prisoners notice on their arrival at a prison, and it is the last thing they notice when they leave. It was, thought the skinny prisoner with images of demons, foul fiends and gargoyles so recently on his mind, the stench of Hell.

Study

Luke 22: 1-6. Judas had spent three years living closely with Jesus and yet he couldn't fight the temptation to betray Him. Judas had a problem with greed and the Devil knew just how to attack. The temptation to turn against Jesus is never far from any of us. How are you guarding yourself today?

Pray

Shamanism, dowsing, paganism, psycho synthesis, Feng Shui, crystals… The period between childhood and adulthood is getting longer for many people. People are staying on in education after the age of sixteen, delaying their entry into work, marriage and the formation of families. During this time many become involved in New Age Movements and parents see these as capturing their children and breaking up families. Pray for young people to find true Christian faith.

FREEDOM THROUGH A
WINDOW

The journey to the Scrubbs had been a long one. More than a hundred miles in the back of a sick-making

diesel van. They had handcuffed him again – as though he would escape! He was barely a child, weighing-in at eight stone.

He could not now understand people who escaped. Why would they bother, unless they had a lot of money to live on? As fugitives they, like him, would not be able to return home, and in order to feed themselves they, like him, would have to get provisions from somewhere. Being wanted by the police, what shops could they enter? How could they get a job to earn money? They may get casual work with a bad employer, like cockle-pickers or illegal immigrants. Who would give them a refuge? Within a week, homeless, they would be starting to starve and desperate for any roof, be it house or hovel, barn or stable, on offer, including even that of a prison cell.

It might be different for those who had a pot of money, like the Great Train robbers, but not for someone like him, a lonely, sad little lad whose parents were ashamed of him, and who would have reported his return home to the police. Where could he go? What place would there be for him? So why did the guards handcuff him in the prison van?

Seated against the interior of the transit van, on a wooden bench alongside other prisoners who were being transferred with him, he simply sat and got sick, staring through the blackened windows. The shadows of houses and stores, and lampposts glided past outside. He needed the lavatory, but there was no provision. He had gone before they left, but his bladder was nervous. He guessed the others were the same. He felt sick. Having inherited a tendency to travel-sickness, his stomach was heaving itself inside out. He was to live with this syndrome for most of his life, discovering thirty years later that he had been suffering not from an inner ear problem but from a curable bowel disorder that blighted his life, recurring at least once a week for over forty years. He squirmed on the floor of the van, sweating and retching uncontrollably. Another prisoner, emotionally wrecked, simply cried all the way to the Scrubbs. They all stared past one another, like on the subway, ignoring one another's presence.

The van slowed to a halt at Du Cane Road. The driver slammed the gear lever into first and lurched through the opened prison gates, which closed behind them with a whirr and clatter. Then, a bang. Then, no sound at all. Thick Portland granite and flint walls kept any sounds from the City of London at bay. Life would go on in the capital. The vanload of prisoners had been safely delivered to their new dispensation of lonely abandonment.

When eventually the doors of the van opened after much scuffling and fevered movement outside in the yard, the prisoners sat rooted to the spot. In the narrow entrance-corridor to the main quad stood eight warders for the four young men. They all looked like hard men, and one had a criss-crossed scarred face. It turned out later that this officer had been thrown from the top of the prison gantry by a group of angry convicts. He had landed on his face in the wire net that stretched across the prison-house arcade just above the first floor. His vengeful little pebble-eyes stared hard at the prisoners as if to say,

'Just do something, you toe-rags. Just do something, and I'll rip your guts out. Just give me one excuse.'

One of them screamed,

'OUT!'

They fell over one another to exit from the van. The lad who had been crying got to his feet, wandered aimlessly from the van and wiped the snot from his nose on his sleeve. The guard belted a mouthful of obscenities at him. He stood with the rest of the prisoners, his terrified eyes wandering around the scene nervously.

The guard walked up to him, poked his nose into the prisoner's face and whispered,

'What's up, lad? There's nothing to be frightened of here at the Scrubbs. We'll tuck you up in bed every night and pat your little head. *That's wot we're 'ere for isn't it?'* He screamed.

'*Wot do yer think this is? A Bloody kindergarten?*'

He strutted back and forth in front of the little band of prisoners with his tail in the air.

'Bloody criminals. Wot's worse, bloody amateur criminals, that's wot! Scum o' the earth, that's wot! People out there...' he motioned with his stick in the general direction of the front wall, '...people out there, they're dead scared of people like you! *Scared! Of you!* Bloody mental, they are...'

His ruminations on the relative levels of comparative fear between people 'in here' and people 'out there' did not have much impact on the band of prisoners lined-up in the corridor, although they did appear to show a level of interest beyond what one would have thought it merited given a different set of circumstances. As it was, it was politic to show an interest when a prison guard was philosophising, however lacking in insight that tirade might be. After all, you did not want to *invite* persecution, did you? His moustache twitched. The skinny prisoner wondered if he were perhaps a repressed homosexual.

He slapped his leg obsessively with his cane, (hmmm... a sadomasochistic repressed homosexual...) and his truncheon poking obviously from under his jacket caused a smile to enter upon the skinny prisoner's face, which he swiftly removed. The guard continued his harangue for five minutes. It was a fine speech, honed to perfection of wit, humour, sarcasm, and accurate Anglo-Saxon invective. As a literary product, it was a work of art. It had been refined and learned by heart. In many respects it had the characteristics of his father's full-flow taunts and emotional twangs.

It did not therefore affect him. It did have an effect on the crying prisoner and on the two hard case prisoners however. The former quailed and sobbed even more, and the hard cases became more and more angry. Either the sobber would go running to the nearest wall and try to climb it with his fingernails, or one of the hard cases was going to flip and attack the guard. This had been, thought the skinny prisoner, what the little show had been designed for. To see what was what and who was who. It was a sort of primitive screening process for troublemakers.

The guard suddenly stopped ranting, and nodded to two of the other guards, who led the group to a small outhouse of large grey breezeblocks. The room was not unlike the rooms at Norwich Prison. The barred gates were the similar, and the smoothly oiled locks could have been in any prison anywhere in the country. There had been an odd and worrying feeling of coming home when the front gate slammed shut. Perhaps this was the first step in the long process of becoming institutionalised.

The skinny prisoner had a sudden irrational rush of euphoria that he was not going to be so unhappy here as he had feared he would be. No, it wasn't going to be so bad after all. Anyway, he thought, it would only be for a few short weeks, and then he'd be on his way to a nice, open borstal.

The little group were led to a long, echoing room. It was decorated in the same colours as the cells in his previous prison. There were scrubbed wooden benches around the walls and in the middle of the room were three large tables painted white gloss. The table-edges were chipped and brown and the corners smoothed and rounded.

Given a choice, most people would avoid large crowds and prefer to be in an open situation, away from too close enforced personal contact. In bus stations and railway waiting rooms all over the world, people compelled by circumstance to be jammed together tend to keep separate from one another. They choose not to communicate, to claim and defend personal space. Perhaps this is some primeval urge for self-defence. Perhaps it demonstrates anxiety arising out of the lack of an agreed power structure within these situations. People do not know who is who and what roles are expected. People often prefer to stand on an open platform in the biting wind and snow than sit with others in a warm railway waiting room. They are more comfortable that way.

There was no opportunity for such niceties in this waiting room. Fifty men and boys were crammed around the benches and around the tables. All were strangers to one another, some wearing the distinctive navy blue and grey of prison uniform and others in civilian clothes. The room was gagging with cigarette smoke – the thick creamy smell of Black Shag mixing with the sickening tar of tailor-made cigarettes. Men and boys sat, stood, or lounged against the walls and propped themselves in corners. There were all kinds of people. The hard case, smouldering still with barely repressed frustration, doubtless planning his security in the upcoming prison experience at the expense of his victims, sulking like an enraged bull; the sobber, quietly crying and bemoaning his fate in a corner of the room; the psychotic prisoner, probably schizophrenic, who ought to be getting some proper health care in hospital for his condition and not in prison getting punishment; the spiv – the one who would sell his grandmother for a cigarette.

Then there would be the pusher of drugs. Cocaine and heroin. At that time convict drug users were paying over a hundred pounds sterling for a 'Joey' (whatever amount that happened to be). Some imprisoned users, many of whom were probably addicts needed up to ten or twelve of these a day. Along with cocaine sales, imagine the amount of money sloshing around in English prisons, and what power these traffickers had in their enclosed world of corruption and violence. Is there any reason to believe that anything except the price has changed to this day? It was not a pretty world, and it was surely not only prisoners who were involved in the trading.

Around the room were the intelligent men who would plough their particular furrow through the prison's social life. There were predatory sexual abusers who would harry the younger prisoners for sexual exploitation, as well as ordinary homosexuals, who were condemned as criminals because of their sexual orientation, and for which some were actually in prison. There was no doubt a smattering of child abusers, or 'sex criminals' whose identity no one yet knew, but when they did, all kinds of frightening violence would be unleashed against them by the cons, occasionally at the instigation of the guards themselves. Among all of these people, the vast majority were youngsters who had volatile or disordered personalities, and who were in this situation mainly as a result of being homeless or outcast from the family. This is not to say that they were not dangerous, or that some of them had not committed the most horrific of crimes, whose incarceration had made life bearable for many people on the outside, not least for their families.

The skinny prisoner found a bit of vacant bench and sat down. The wait lengthened to seventeen hours. It seemed like an eternity. It was dark outside when the prison guard eventually came in and started calling out names from a list. One by one the names were called and small groups of men huddled quietly out of the room. Eventually, when the room was almost empty, the skinny prisoner's name was called. He lined up with some other lads and followed the guard into a huge courtyard.

An old oak tree raised its uppermost twigs above the prison wall, proclaiming freedom! In the still air, the tree stood as a silent sentry against the grey sky. An aeroplane sputtered overhead on its way to or from Heathrow, little red and green lights flashing in the darkening air. The sound of the engines disappeared, and another began to sound in the distance. It was a busy airport, whose sounds would provide the audio background for the whole of his time spent at Wormwood Scrubbs. The group walked two abreast across the courtyard. A black and grey flint wall loomed ahead. At regular intervals along the wall were small black cavities. They formed four rows from one end of the eighty-foot high wall to the other. These were cell windows. Someone banged his chamber pot against the bars and shouted. His voice carried across the yard and hung in the still evening air. Another aeroplane circled overhead, mocking his captivity.

As they approached the wall, the individual cell windows could be seen clearly. There were little pallid faces at some of them. He imagined their suffering. They were right in front of him now. It raised a tear to his eye. Maybe self-pity as well as empathetic compassion. There were occasional moans and shouts from the cell windows that could only be heard from up close. Chamber pots banged against steel window-bars. Helpless powerlessness against the unhearing darkness. Despair and hopelessness. Wormwood! He had read in the philosophers about the ghost in the machine, but here was a living example of flesh bodies in cages of steel, nuts and bolts. Predating Star Trek, here was a vision of the Borg! Aeroplanes overhead continually taunting reminded the prisoner in his lonely cell of speeding commuter trains taking men and women to their warm homes, warm children and warm husbands and wives. The pity of it all. Was there not another way of dealing with crime in the community?

He didn't know what he was doing or why he was feeling the way he was. Maybe it had been the short spell of freedom he'd had the previous day. Maybe it was the sudden reminder of the reality of his imprisonment, the reminder of its endlessness – he had been given an open-ended term, so did not have a date to look forward to. Why was he weeping as he walked across the courtyard? For them? For himself? For something else? Pity? Tragedy? Humanity? Why?

God knows he did not know. And to this day he still does not know. The whole business was just sad.

The five-barred gate swung open.

'Fifteen.'

'Troublemakers?'

'Nope.'

'Right. Get 'em banged up.'

It was good to be back in the safety of a single cell again. Good to be alone, to have a bit of a cry; to read something and have a sleep. It had been a heavy day.

The friendly cell door creaked and he went in. It smelled of the same stale faeces and urine as every other cell. There was the same colour scheme, only a bit more faded and dirty. Three of the small windows had been smashed and the glass eye in the door had been poked through, so that there was a keen draught entering the room. The ceiling was thick with yellow dust and cigarette smoke and the floor cried out for scrubbing.

He thanked the guard, who left the door open and went away. It was cocoa time. He went to the door and peeked out. A guard shouted from the other end of the gantry '*Get your effing head in!*' and he pulled his head back in to the cell.

A train of Trustee cons with red bands round their left arms arrived with a bucket of cocoa. They filled his mug and handed him a very hard waxen bun. He banged his own door shut, and began to think about his departure for borstal. A few weeks and he would be leaving the confines of the Scrubbs and headed for the green fields of an open borstal, working on the land in the good fresh air.

Suddenly the voice of a woman lifted into the still air. He was sure it was a young woman. He listened. His heart began to palpitate. He did not reflect on why this was, but perhaps it was because this was the last thing you would expect in a male prison late at night. The sound recurred. It was from outside.

He climbed onto his chair and strained at the high window. There in the street, under a burning street lamp was a courting couple. They were kissing. She laughed privately and intimately, for her friend's joke. It was a very strange experience. There were ordinary free people walking down the street as though there were no prison towering above them.

He stayed there, propped against the window for a very long time, pretending that he was part of what was happening before his eyes and not shut away in a cell. He just watched people going by. It was both sad and joyful. When he finally got down from the window he

ached all over. He had experienced freedom through a window, and there was still the bed to make.

Study

Isaiah 53: 1-6. This is probably the most famous passage from the Old Testament talking about the death of Jesus. The suffering of Jesus Christ provides amazing salvation for you today. Are you in a 'wormwood-like' place? Or are you thinking of someone you know who is in a bad place? Ask God to speak to you today as you read.

Pray

Pray for those in strange or unfamiliar situations. Pray for those who are looking to a future of pain and suffering with fear and uncertainty. Pray for the persecuted and for those who persecute them, and for all whose suffering makes them lonely and isolated. Pray for all lovers under all lampposts, and for all who walk near prisons.

ASSAULT OF FREEDOM

Prison suffering doesn't show. It is emotional, psychological, and spiritual. It is internal. It is the pain of deprivation of liberty. Physical pain is more easily detectable. A head injury, though tragic and painful is clear to see, whereas an injury of the spirit, caused by being deprived of human company for weeks and months on end does not show itself. A tortured mind is less obvious than a tortured body. Crying out for companionship is a sad and lonely, futile occupation. Screaming in agony over a newly acquired cut or burn is not sad, but normal. The issue is one of sympathy. A wounded spirit draws no empathy, and demands a lot of committed caring from any would-be healer.

It is a good thing that to some extent the human spirit adjusts itself to this kind of wounding. After a few weeks in prison, suffering these shocks to the mind, a person usually becomes accustomed and is able to adjust to it. A resigned attitude helps to mitigate the pain. However, there are those who will never get used to it, and who are destined never to heal. These are those who end up in a bad way, finding it difficult to harden themselves. These are the cell suicides.

For the skinny prisoner, it took seven weeks before he found that resignation was the better way. A prison is no place to start trying to change the world. The mark of a mature convict is that he can approach his sentence with cool resolution and complete his term without disturbing the calm of his surface. He can do his time without too many shocks. He can settle down and cruise through as many years as is necessary. He comes into prison, gets friendly with the guards, and develops mutually supportive relationships with key convicts and trustees. Before long, he obtains a safe and comfortable job in the laundry, library or administration department. This way, before he has time to reflect on the tragedy of his situation, he is at the end of his sentence and due for release within a few months time. For this prisoner, a year or two years is 'not long now before my release', whereas for a young prisoner, two years is a lifetime. This is one reason why the young prisoner suffers so much. Time is relative. It is also true that the older a person is, the faster time passes.

It's easy for the mature convict, of course. However, in the process of wasting his life he is not learning anything or developing in any way. He has closed his mind and become insensitive. He'll never reform. On the other hand, who would not take the easy way out if they knew of one? Who would choose to suffer torture if he could find a way to avoid it? Living and surviving is always costly. Either you choose to suffer the pain and develop it into something worthwhile, or you choose to lie dormant and wake unchanged.

Living in a cell thus became less difficult for the skinny prisoner. Sometimes he would open his mind and suffer, and other times he would close his spirit down and let the time fly by. He was aware, however, that it was during those times of painful openness that he learned the most, and that his spirit grew. It was then that he discovered the most precious things about himself and the world around him. However, it was painful and he didn't do it often.

Sometimes there would be work to do. Making B.O.A.C. travelling bags and little dolls for a local retailer passed the time and engaged some motor skills. Now and again one of the prisoners' bells would ring and the guard could be heard unlocking the cell to see what the problem was. Usually it was someone wanting to use the lavatory, and other times it was just a need for human company – a few words from another person, just to touch base with humanity – just for the sake of it. Very little ever happened. There were no riots and few fights. Someone would sing *Danny Boy* or *Green Grass of Home*. The stacked aircraft circled overhead every three minutes preparing to land, and the occasional jingle of keys could be heard along the gantry.

Unpredictably, a team of bored guards ordering the men to undergo a medical inspection – for which they would have to be marched to the Medical Block, would open the cell door. Other times the cells would be opened singly, one-by-one for a cell search. The former involved a perfunctory trousers down and cough and back to the cell, and the latter a thorougoing disruption of the whole of the contents of the cell. Clothing, personal effects, toiletries, bedding and everything else that was moveable, got thrown out and tossed around – in the case of the skinny prisoner – in a vain attempt to find illicit drugs, money, tobacco, alcohol or anything else that ought not to be there. This prisoner never had anything illegal. He was barely a child, and spent the three years of his incarceration in a state of constant terror, always fearing that the worst might happen, and often finding that it did. He would not step over anyone's lines. He lacked the courage, and despised himself to the degree that he counted himself worthy of no favours or privileges.

He *was* the scum of the earth. The long-impressed message had gotten through many years ago, and his imprisonment had merely confirmed its truth. In this prison nothing ever happened. The days came and went, and the only break from routine was the half-an-hour of tannoi radio on Saturday evening, which piped swing music through the prison speakers whether you wanted it or not. More often than not, it was a relief when it ended, mainly because it was an intrusion of the outside world into the cut-off isolation of the prison routine. It broke hearts. Which, thought the cynical Roy, had been its purpose.

There is boredom, when there is nothing to engage the mind, and there is a point beyond boredom, when the mind does not wish to be engaged. Post-boredom restlessness comes first, followed by weeping and cursing and dribbling and snotting, followed by an almost catatonic state in which a man simply sits in his chair and does nothing. He might be dead, or he might be a wooden statue. He may occasionally, in this state, rap his knuckles into the table or drum rhythmically with the tips of his fingers. He just sits, and there would be little to distinguish him from a cursory glance from a patient in a psychiatric hospital on some calming drug. He does nothing and thinks nothing and feels nothing.

Perhaps for the Buddhists, or those who practise mediation or Yoga this is considered to be some 'higher spiritual state'. I wouldn't know. But whatever else it is, it is a state beyond boredom, and it is a non-being, non-feeling, pain-reliever that brings a temporary relief to the agony of confinement. It is a spiritual morphine, beyond self-pity. It is a mental vacuum. It is the other side of living, beyond humanity. It is the place where Jesus went after his crucifixion. It is hell's ante-room. It was the calm before the skinny prisoner's storm.

Such was the main part of his stay in Wormwood Scrubbs. He had read through all the bound editions of *Punch* magazine, many Agatha Christies and countless other pulp authors during that two months in the Scrubbs. He had not yet become sufficiently desperate or bored to read through more challenging books. That would come later in this strange university course. By the time he left, he had completed three months imprisonment, but his actual term of service had not yet begun. That did not happen until the first day spent in an actual borstal. The three months did not count, or come off his sentence. It was time that did not exist.

He reflected wryly that it had never been known for a borstal boy to be released less than eight months into his time. The sentence had been for nine months to three years. The judge had said that the length of time served would be decided by the good behaviour of the prisoner. It had not occurred to him that some guards favoured some prisoners and some governors were more lenient than others, and that most of the people who worked for the service didn't give a damn to care enough about the lads in their charge. Few would actually notice good behaviour. What they *did* notice was personal inconvenience, and what they *were* capable of was revenge. They had the power to delay a prisoner's release for as long as they liked, and there was no mechanism for monitoring or controlling it. The harsh fact was that you needed to be a good manipulator so that you could get in with the guards to ensure an early release. Doubtless there were also those who had special talents to offer to certain guards, but the skinny prisoner had only rumour and no actual evidence of that.

Many prisoners handed this sentence were released within a period of about eighteen months. This was the expected average among them, when they had the opportunity of talking about it. Some got out earlier, but eighteen months was a reasonable target to set yourself. That was with everything going well, and no trouble. It was too long. It was a precious year and a half of teenage life. He had difficulty in understanding what was right in keeping him in detention. Try as he might, he had no way of understanding what gave them the right to deprive him of his freedom. He had admitted to the crimes he had committed, and he could see that. But what he could not accept was the harshness of the punishment. It did not fit the crime, since the crime had arisen out of his psychological, familial, and social pain rather than any innate evil.

He saw no difference between those who had condemned him and himself. If anything, he thought, they were more criminal than he was. After all, what had he done? Borrowed a few motorcars, entered a few houses, stolen a few trinkets. What had society lost because of his activities? A few trinkets, a few drops of petrol and a spot of white paint on a few window-ledges. That was all. He was sure that people who appeared to be decent and law-abiding were perpetrating much bigger crimes than his every day.

It was in this frame of mind that he had decided that at the first opportunity he would escape. He was not angry. For the first time, he saw himself as an individual being targeted by the system. He wanted freedom, and had decided to get it. The essential element of that freedom was, 'now', for what else could it be? In his heart, he knew that escaping would not work, even if he were successful in getting away. But he determined that he would try. It was as simple and unreasonable and senseless as that.

As those dreadful boring months drew slowly to a close, having little else to think about, he became more and more inflamed with the lust for freedom. Then the Assistant Governor summoned him to his office, and told him that he had finally been allocated a borstal. It was called Gains Hall and was set in the beautiful countryside of Cambridgeshire. He would be leaving at the earliest opportunity. He did not ask for a date, for there was no such thing as 'immediately' in the English prison system. He thanked the Assistant Governor and restrained himself from kissing the Chief Officer on his way from the office.

In his cell, he wanted to dance, like the first time he had kissed a girl. He had skipped all the way home from the playground and slept fitfully, waking regularly to taste that kiss over and over again. The cell was too small for dancing, so he got up on his chair, stared out of the window, saw the couple kissing, as they always did, and surveyed the chimney-tops and the twinkling lights and stars. Soon, he would be cuddled and surrounded with freedom. He was filled with joy, because he knew now for sure that he would escape. Gains Hall was an open borstal. It had no wall. He'd be out within a couple of hours of arriving. The two weeks after his interview with the Assistant Governor flew past, and the day of rejoicing came.

It was a day that had been worth all the tears and indignities. He had become wiser now by far. Every sacrifice he had made – even the damned tattoo that would mark him for life – the judges and probation officers and social workers who had all wanted a piece of him, to put him right, to show him what to do and how to do it, interfering in his life and demanding his soul, prying in to his family and making his father even angrier than he had been before the family became involved with them. How his father had hidden the fire of that anger from them all, he could never understand. This was why he had such contempt for them, because despite their authority and intrusions, they lacked the insight to get behind his father's deceitfulness. They were basically ignorant. On that joyful day, all of these things came to his mind, and steeled his determination.

Had the suffering been worthwhile? Yes, it had. Indeed it had been worthwhile. Forced upon him, though. It had not been through his choosing. Their justice had simply demanded a borstal sentence. But it was their justice. It was justice such that decreed his sentence had not yet even begun. Four months of imprisonment and it had counted for nothing. Their sentence was only now about to begin. He was going to escape, and make up for those four months. The escape itself, he had decided, would be the balancing of the scales, no matter what happened subsequently.

He had read somewhere that a child who is treated fairly will respond fairly and a child who is treated unjustly will repay the same. He will boil with resentment if he is powerless, and break the bonds. He felt himself to be, in that sense, a child of the state. The parent-state, full of good intentions without doubt, had treated him unjustly. He thus resented the state. He became quite calm, not wanting to indicate the upheaval of euphoria that had arisen within. He had become a model of sweet obedience and politeness. It was probably feelings similar to these that were later to inspire other young men, under the tutelage of political and gangster mentors, to rebel against the state and commit ghastly terrorist crimes.

It had not occurred to him, because his thinking had taken place entirely in the theoretical world, in which the landscape was thoughts and not realities that he would require somewhere to escape *to*. Some physical place where he could actually go to. Freedom had been for him an *idea*, but he had not considered the practical implications of being on the run. The idea that had engaged his mind was simply *getting out* - to tear himself away from the punishing establishment. It had been more an assertion of his personal freedom within than a desire for actual independence in the community. He knew he couldn't get away with it, but that what was important was to say that he was free, an individual. If he had thought he could get away with it, he wouldn't have bothered. Deep down he was protesting because he wanted the system that captivated him to accept him and to understand his situation and to respond with love. He did not know this at the time, and would not understand it until decades later. It was thus a futile task, which he could not know.

The guard unlocked the door and let it swing open. The skinny prisoner collected his bedding and clattered down the cast iron staircases to the ground floor. On the way down he could feel eyes tracing his progress through the peepholes.

'Cheerio, Jacko! See yer in Dartmoor.' He said chirpily to the hole in the door of No. 28. The last sound he heard on that first visit to Wormwood Scrubbs was the sound of a kicked pot clanging across a flagstone floor and crashing against the door. He exited the cellblock into the cold morning air. He was led past the office. The guard had his ear to the radio. It was August Seventh, and he was nineteen – the average age of the boys given leave by Congress on that day to engage in all out slaughter of the people of North Vietnam without a formal declaration of war. It was a world he knew lacked justice, his own little world being but a reflection of the wider scene.

The van was waiting. They had not bothered to handcuff this group of prisoners since they were destined for an open institution with no walls. They were a docile bunch and no trouble was expected. What a glorious day it was. Cold and sharp, but a gorgeous sun. The guards wore civilian clothes and the van had windows in the sides. The prisoners had been given civilian clothes, and for the entire world they looked like a group of happy psychiatric patients out on a day trip with a charity organisation.

He absentmindedly flicked his wrist to look at the time. Instead of a watch he saw the tattoo, the symbol of his filthiness; the visible reminder of what his true situation was. A prisoner on his way to borstal. His final teenage year, and it was to be spent in prison. His civilian clothes were crumpled and creased where they had been thrown in a heap in a suitcase. His hair was unfashionably cropped. It was the days of the Beatles and long hair was the fashion. John Lennon had just bought himself a mansion in Weybridge, and the Beatles started to use marijuana with Bob Dylan. It would not be long before the skinny prisoner would feel the effects of this cultural sea change and experience the paranoia of cannabis himself. He was conscious of his naked skull and flapping ears.

He rolled a substantial cigarette to celebrate. That night he would escape. Any doubt he may have had was now quashed. The open windows in the van had done it. He wouldn't be a prisoner any longer than he could help.

Derek sat next to him. They had agreed to escape together that night. It felt good to have a comrade. The agreement they had made gave them a wonderful bond of fellowship. They both rolled a cigarette, but Derek offered one of his own. This was unheard of in prison circles. Tobacco was the gold of the prison economy. No one ever gave tobacco away. He took a match – a full-sized and un-split match, and set it to the cigarette. Zip! The match gloried into brilliant light. They caught one another's eyes and shared the secret. Yes. Tonight they would be free.

He closed his eyes as the rubber rumbled along the open road. He could feel the palpitations of his heart through his chest. His spirit was also bouncing. It was a good feeling. Eventually Gains Hall came in to view. It was concealed behind a copse of trees and shrubs. There was a long, sweeping drive, three or four small buildings, and a larger, longer building behind them. All of these were prefabricated, and there was a tiny estate of brick-built houses further up the road, nearer the centre of the facility. This, he guessed, was where the staff lived. There were cars in the driveways. Handy for later, he reflected.

The whole thing struck him as being a holiday or lax boot camp, where everyone had fun, only with rules. He wondered where the swimming pool was. This was not imprisonment. It was a holiday! For a second, he wondered if he really wanted to escape. Well, 'escape'. It could hardly be called that, since all that was necessary was to walk down the street and keep going.

He knew he was deluding himself, though. It would not be a holiday camp. The plain glass windows might not have bars, but there were bars all right. The new white paint and the picket fences might convey the impression of gentility and civilisation, but he knew differently. There was a power structure and a punishment regime here, just as there was in a closed institution. These things might impress the casual visitor or the local politician, or even the people who lived in the neighbouring villages, but they did not convince the borstal boy with several months of un-counted imprisonment behind him.

He wondered how many nice men and women had tried to make the lot of the prisoner a little easier. He had read about a man called Howard who had done a lot for prisoners, though he couldn't see it. Things must have been pretty bad before if this bloke had done as much as they said. He had an inscription on his statue in St.Paul's Cathedral in London,

'This extraordinary man had the fortune

to be honoured whilst living,

In the manner which his virtues deserved:

He received the thanks

Of both houses of the British and Irish Parliaments,

For his eminent services rendered to his country

and to mankind.'

There had doubtless been speeches in Parliament and flowing sentences in the statute books. How many had tried? How few? And how few must have succeeded, from the state of things thus far! At grass roots most of their work meant nothing – at least to this prisoner. Good people, yes, and well meaning too. But they hadn't fully understood. How could they? The simple fact that they had power meant that they were alienated from a real understanding of the prisoner's plight. They had never been locked up in a cell with no hope of release, in the confines of a stink from a chamber-pot used by three men whilst being tortured by a psychopath. Unlike him, they had never been convinced of their status as the scum of the earth.

Trees stood all around, and tenderly cut privet hedging stood sentinel at every street junction and driveway. Across the field an ancient tractor chugged and spluttered half-a-dozen furrows with its plough fitment attached. This would be one of the inmates at work.   An inmate would also have done the hedge trimming.   Four lads dug cheerfully at the edge of a well-trimmed lawn.   The guard's children looked on from the bay window.   Slaves of Her Majesty at Her Majesty's pleasure.   They would have been just as happy in a cell.   The open freedom served only as a deep reminder to him of their enslavement.   Not only as individuals, but as members of an English outcaste, whose family names rolled down the centuries of criminal history.   All that pleasant environment.   But what life could they expect?   Unemployment for life, and at most a casual labouring job whilst their muscles lasted.   They wanted physical freedom but they would never have it.   They longed for a new world in which they did not have to obey the dictates of their class and culture.   But it was not a thing that was destined for them.   It was a dream.   Their children would inherit their unemployment and their despair.

Like a fool, he did not himself see that it was a dream at the time. But he was young and had not yet lived, and it was the Sixties when everything was possible. After all, hadn't John Lennon just bought himself a mansion…? He really believed that freedom was possible; that it could be found. He decided then and there that he wouldn't wait. He would go as soon as darkness fell. Derek would have to make his own decision.

Study

Isaiah. 53: 7-12. The cross was real and the suffering of Jesus is a historical reality. It is hard to face up to how awful it was, but the results of sin are horrible suffering and death. Jesus went through all this because He wants to save you. What is your response to Him today?

Pray

Pray for all who are searching for a key to freedom, but try the wrong doors. Pray for all who use inappropriate people and things to find release from captivity. Pray for people seeking release from all kinds of incarceration, emotionally, psychologically, morally, socially, culturally, ethnically, mentally and in terms of their faith.

THE WRONG KEY

As it turned out, Derek and Roy were consigned to different huts. This was probably deliberate, their having arrived from the same prison in the same van, sitting on the same seat and on the same day. It was possible they may have been conspiring together, especially after such a long time in close confinement in the prison system. An open prison was too much of a temptation to anyone with an ounce of spirit. Best to keep them apart for a couple of days.

Thus the race, such as it was, almost came to grief at the first hurdle. A means had to be found for them to communicate to arrange the time and place of their departure. By one of those odd turns of coincidence, whilst queuing to receive a change of clothes from the Matron's (yes, there was a Matron) office, he noticed Derek was at the head of the queue. He walked past and whispered,

'Half an hour after lights out, back of my dormitory.'

He nodded discreetly to indicate that he understood and would be there. Was there a trace of hesitation and regret in his eyes? If so, the skinny prisoner elected to ignore it. He failed in his attempt to reassure himself as he raced to catch Derek before he disappeared into his dormitory. But Matron stood at the doorway, passing bundles of clothes to prisoners. He stopped, turned around, and went back to his hut.

All that afternoon and evening he worried. What if Derek wasn't there? He wondered if he had the courage to go it alone. Where was the nearest town? He did not know St. Neot's was a couple of miles away, and if he had, he would still not have known where it was in the country or in relation to anywhere else. Apart from his travels in prison vans, he had only once ever been out of his home county, and that had been to the neighbouring county, Norfolk, when he was eight. Which way would he go? Somehow the idea of two people together made all these awful questions unimportant. The thought of him being alone made them into enormous obstacles. Perhaps if Derek did not turn up, he would abandon the whole idea and knuckle down to serving his time.

At half past ten, the lights went out. At eleven o'clock, the skinny prisoner got out of bed, crept to the door, and slipped into the darkness. Had the door been open because there were dogs on the loose in the grounds? Surely not. The door had opened without a sound. The garden was cold but not too cold to bear. He should have put a large coat on. The air was clear and the three-quarter moon was up. There was not a cloud in the sky. The scent of the newly cut lavender hedge wafted across the facility on a light breeze.

He made his way to the rear of the dormitory, half-hoping that Derek had decided not to go. He had put on some heavy working boots for walking across the fields and streams. He waited for five minutes and Derek appeared from behind the hut, creeping along the wall to join him. He had come. They grinned at each other. What was in their individual minds? They started off towards the long, curved gravel driveway. They had seen a major road on the way in and decided to make for it. That way, the might get a lift to the nearest town, although it was unlikely they would be picked up this late at night. They could have been vagrants, or criminals even! Both prisoners had stuffed their bedclothes with pillows to give the impression they were soundly in their beds, but they did not think it would fool them for long.

In fact, back at the borstal, no one was bothered about escapees. They had had many new lads leave on the first night, and were used to it. All it did was to inform the choices that had already been made by the prison authorities. Some prisoners who were likely to benefit from an open situation, but who might need to be confined within walls were sent to open borstals to see if they needed confinement. These prisoners clearly did. All they were doing was behaving like the rats in the social engineer's maze. They did not know that, of course.

In their own little world of fantasy, they ran, crouched down beneath the windows, toward the drive. Suddenly they froze. There was someone coming. They dived into the privet hedge and lay flat on the damp earth, their hearts pounding. They were enjoying the suspense, the excitement of the chase. A guard rode by on his bicycle a hundred yards down the road, whistling in the breeze. He got off his bike and walked towards them. Thinking they had already been caught, Roy began to stand up and surrender himself. But the guard turned on his heel and walked briskly off in the opposite direction. The two escapees looked at each other and decided it would be too risky going by the road, and that the best plan was to go across the fields. If the guard were the first of the new shift, there would be others along pretty soon. It was too big a gamble to go that way. The fields' route was agreed, and they set off across heavy clay soil towards a clump of trees about two miles distant. It was already a mad idea, but there was no going back. The further they went, the further their common sense retreated from them, until there was no going back. The light of the moon picked them out as a spotlight, and they hurried towards the clump of trees, beyond which was the main road. Keeping close to the shrubbery they had no problems with getting through the borstal grounds. Nothing stirred. There were no dogs and no guards. In front of them lay the open fields. The lack of cloud cover meant that they would have to go the whole way in the relative light. They hoped no one would be looking in that direction, and set off in to the first field.

The ground was damp and sticky, deep with ploughed-up mud. After struggling for a few yards they both realised that this was hopeless. They would have to remove their boots and go barefoot. The borstal was still in full view, and they could be seen from a mile off, clearly depicted by the moonlight against the horizon. A casual glance from a bored guard or officer's wife would betray them. The single cloud in the sky drew back from the moon, spotlighting their position in the middle of the field. They dived to the ground, covering their faces with coats, and lay there for a full thirty minutes waiting for the next cloud. Time was running out and something had to be done. Soon there would be a routine inspection of the dormitories. Their absence could be noticed. They couldn't afford to wait any longer. They grabbed their boots and made a dash for the clump of trees. It must have provided refuge for hundreds of escapees over the years. Relaxing for a few minutes in the shelter of the wood, the congratulated one another for getting this far. They had made a break for it, and there was no going back. Neither knew what the future might hold, but it would include some excitement and some freedom if little else.

Putting their boots back on, they started off across the remaining fields. They had smoked a whole civilian cigarette each. It was best to keep away from the road if possible, and they ran along the verge, diving into the grass every time a car passed by. Ahead of them they could just make out the silhouette of a bridge, which would take them to the major road, where they might hitch a lift of steal a car. A police car was parked in the lay-by, and they took a large diversion to avoid it. They had probably been told about the two borstal boys who were roaming about. This involved another detour across muddy fields, and by this time they were becoming tired. They would have given anything for a cup of coffee. Soon dazed and out of breath, the fleeing couple sat down and lit up another cigarette. After another long walk and another police car, they eventually found the road. The village of St. Neots lay nestled in the dark folds of the night, and someone had left his car parked in the drive. They had gone almost in a circle. However, they had not been caught. The car was in a secluded spot and far enough away from the house to be started without disturbing the householders. Every footstep on the gravel drive sounded like a bad of crisps in a cinema. After prizing the door open, they got in and pushed it gently to the road, where they gunned it to life and careered off towards the centre of the village.

Sharing yet another civilian cigarette – the last one – they drove the little vehicle down the A1 road and discussed where they would go. They had the idea of going to Southampton. They could jump on a ship and get across to France, out of the reach of the village copper and the open borstal guard. Neither of them had ever been abroad, but there was something magical about the idea of a foreign country. Belying their behaviour and language, and their desperate situation, they really were children. Their ideas of freedom and escape, and their lack of plans for survival were the fantasy theme for a boys' story, not the real plans of two actual lives. It is possible to understand their dreams from the point of view of children, but what is puzzling is how, later, after their capture, the adult authorities reacted in such a way that they considered the children's behaviour to be culpable, blame-able, criminal, and punishable. Looking back, it seems odd that the punishment for this 'crime', by middle-class righteous people, and the informal prison courts system, was to be as harsh, retributive, and adult as it actually was.

The car engine spluttered. Out of fuel. They would have to find another quickly. That was not a problem, and they dumped the first and stole the second. Neither realised that this was to provide a clear trail for the police to follow. They had been gone well over two hours and the police would certainly be on their trail by now. If ever they did return, it would be because they had been captured. The police, who would be alerted by now, would be after them, and they had to take some kind of cover – find some kind of shelter. They realised that they had been leaving a trail, and decided to steal another car, drive them both for a few miles and then dump the first and carry on in the second vehicle. This would throw the police off their trail, they thought. In the rush, Derek couldn't remember where the light-switch was, so the car was dumped in a ditch with the headlamps glowing. Great thinking!

It was a magnificently clear night. A dew had begun to settle and the headlamps of the new vehicle cleared a path before them. This was the true taste of freedom. This was what it had all been for. It was unbelievably peaceful, and the rumble of the rubber on tarmac was hypnotic. The road streamed peacefully beneath the wheels, and the two boys fell in to silence.

It was not long before the peace was disturbed by the flashing of headlamps in the rear-view mirror. It was some fool driving with his headlamps on, wanting to overtake. Roy put his foot on the accelerator, thinking that the other driver wanted a race. There was no way he was going to get past unless he had a more powerful engine and a clear space on the road ahead. Derek put his finger up at the rear window and the driver continued flashing his lights, keeping pace easily. Four or five miles down the road, Derek quietly said that it might be the police. He could see a blue flashing light.

This was not what either of them wanted to hear.

'Pigs!' He said.

A chilling tension ran through the skinny escapee's body like an electric shock, numbing his reactions. He became acutely aware of the road, and just as when he had come off the scooter and crashed into the street lamp, everything seemed to move in slow motion. The silhouetted of trees and buildings and road signs flitted past as in a silent movie. The white lines in the centre of the road became machine-gun pellets, stuttering dead centre between the front wheels of the car. Side to side they swung as the shining black eel of the tarmac glided from left to right beneath them. It was the police. They had been discovered.

The car surged forward with reserves of power as the skinny escapee's adrenaline levels lifted. Heart palpitating, head in a whirl, they had stolen a powerful car. The owner would have a bit of polishing to do when they had finished with it. Grit and water spinned off the road as they sped along the dual carriageway. A junction sailed gently into view, and the needle was hovering at 85 miles an hour.

A small white family saloon cruised at a gentle thirty miles an hour past the junction opening. The stolen car shot past and twisted itself into the turning, bringing it to the rims of the offside wheels. Ahead lay a narrow road, offering the police no opportunity to get past. A sharp turning offered itself on the left and the car threatened to turn over as it took the turn. The narrow lane led on to a major road. It began to rain and they could not find the wiper switch. The resulting circus of oncoming cars dazzled the two escapees into near blindness, and the incessant burning of the headlamps of the police in the rear view mirror added to their discomfort. Until then, it had been exciting. A dream world like on the television. Noble, almost.

A memory flashed in to the skinny escapee's mind. One of the lads at the Scrubbs had told him a tale. The police had chased him along Oxford Street in London. His only way of escape had been to turn and go in the opposite direction. He had done this by jamming the handbrake on and jerking the steering wheel hard to the right. The effect had been – he said – to turn the vehicle around on a pinhead, so it was facing the opposite direction. The lad who had told this story was a 'driver' so he knew what he was talking about. He had never seen it done, and he wondered whether he should put his neck on the block. Had the driver been lying? It seemed there was only one thing to do. He was about to execute the manoeuvre, when more police closed in from the sides of the vehicle, their lights blazing.

They drove forward, storming through the village and out the other side into open country. Now was the time to give it a try and pray that it would work. But it wasn't possible. The opportunity did not present itself. Two police cars lay behind them, side by side. It would have been carnage. Increased speed was the only option. The needle indicated from thirty-to-ninety. The police stuck fast. There was no way out. The skinny escapee began to see himself as the skinny prisoner in Wormwood Scrubbs again. He saw tall grey and flint walls and smelled the emptying of chamber pots at slopping-out time.

A long stretch of open road offered itself to the speeding wheels. He took the offer, spurred on by his memory of the Scrubbs. Dimly in the distance a small dark shape lay across the road. It became clearer as they approached the roadblock. Taking the grass shoulder, it held, and the car stayed upright, negotiating the barrier. They had made it. It would take quite a while to sort that lot out. All that was needed now was a side turning and a bit of luck. Searching the roadside for a turning, none came.

Ahead in a lay-by a red-and-white police car waited silently. Like a spider in its web, it remained completely motionless. The fly approached with increasing speed. Maybe it could break through the web. The police car waited. They had no choice but to overtake. Suddenly all the tyres burst. The stolen car slowed on it wheel rims and dragged itself to a halt. The grass verge roused itself up before them and a barbed fence reared up in front of the window and caught the car as it plunged off the road. The engine stalled in top gear. Silence came and settled around them.

The police approached the vehicle. They had done all they could to escape. There was nothing else they could do. A blue light pulsed through the wet darkness.

If these two children had had guns, and this was a sobering reality about teenage criminals, they would have used them at that point. Trapped and frightened and not knowing if or how badly they had been injured, they might have done anything.

Knowing that the police had truncheons and knew how to use them, the two boys got out of the car and lay down prone on the grass. There was no more escaping. Dragged roughly to their feet, the two escapees were escorted, handcuffed, to the police van. The expected crushing blow of a truncheon never happened.

'Ah, well, lad, back to the nick then, eh?'

His voice was compassionate, gentle and kind. Not recognising the two new lads – they were not members of his usual clientele, but from another part of the country - the tubby officer gazed with concern written on a gentle and handsome face. He wanted to hate the copper but couldn't. Nor could he put it together that a policeman – his natural enemy – could be a good man.

If the chase had pumped excess adrenaline through his veins, freezing his sense of fear, the friendliness of the policeman had numbed his understanding. They handed cigarettes around and sat chatting in the van as they made their way to the police station.

Once there, the sergeant's wife cooked them a meal and left the cell boor open. They must have provided it out of their own store. The skinny prisoner felt like a heel, already regretting the thoughts he had experienced during the heat of the chase.

At half past nine the following morning, a van came with two Scrubbs guards in it. They bundled the two captives into the back and took a leisurely drive back to the prison.

The skinny prisoner's heart sank. Anywhere but there. He slept fitfully, suffering the sickness from his constantly present stomach condition during the return journey. He couldn't face another journey like the one from Norwich Prison two months earlier.

He had already learned that sleep was an effective narcotic, and had used it often. It was ironic. Earlier the day before, he had left the Scrubbs filled with anticipation and joy. Then, he had felt the poison of a desire for freedom seeping into his heart. It had begun to spread until it had filled his mind and driven out all reason and sense. Then, when he made the break, the poison seemed to transform into nectar, and he had sped towards freedom at its insistence. But what was 'freedom'?

In the early hours of the new day the freedom that had promised so much had become a cancer that had grown and spread, endangering life and soul on the open road. It was no longer pleasurable. All it had left was the empty space where joy had been and hope had found its home. It had eaten its fill and was sated. Joy was embittered and all hope was gone.

It was back to prison. Back to that dark, grey, hateful place that stunk of faeces and urine. Back to the boredom and grinding poverty of social contact. What had he learned from the experience? That he was a fool; that he was sad and powerless and without hope; that he was an idiot; that he had failed to make a plan, and that freedom did not exist unless you had money and somewhere to go.

The guard kindly offered the two lads a cigarette. Grateful, they sucked the smoke into their lungs.

'Thanks, brother.' Said the skinny captive.

Study

Luke 18: 31-34. Jesus explains to His disciples what is going to happen in Jerusalem but they couldn't understand. God's way of doing things is different from ours. How difficult is that for you to handle? How easy do you find it to trust Him?

Pray

Pray for all those who seek inappropriate thrills at the expense of other people. Bring before the Lord the needs of those given authority to maintain just law and civil order. Through prayer, enlist spiritual help to those who appear to be opposed to one another by class, geography, culture or history, to come together in mutual understanding and love.

SOLITARY CONFINEMENT

After his return to Wormwood Scrubbs he was placed in a cell with a small red lamp burning continually in the ceiling. He had been before the board of visitors, who had held their kangaroo court in the Governor's Office and sentenced him to three days bread-and-water to be added to his borstal sentence. This happened in the absence of *habeas corpus* or a defending barrister. That was the way things were done. Once you were beyond the legal process, no records were available, so no evidence existed.

The Habeas Corpus Act was passed by Parliament in 1679. It promised that a person detained by the authorities would be brought before a court of law so that the legality of the detention may be examined. In times of social unrest, Parliament had the power to suspend Habeas Corpus. Clearly it is here being suspended when dealing with the punishment of children in England's prison system.

It was overkill, and they need not have bothered anyway. It was sufficient punishment for him to have been returned to the Scrubbs.

What can be said about the bread and water punishment? It was something to eat and drink. There were people in the outside world, in England's pleasant land, who would happily deny prisoners even that much. Bread and water was not a luxury, and who would expect to be rewarded for escaping? The trick for survival and sanity was to treat it as being on a diet, or religious fasting.

The dreadful thing was not the bread and water, it was having to spend another two months in that rat-hole of an institution. Part of the problem was that you were unable to make any friends or contact with another individual on a friendly social level. Even if it were physically possible, whom could you trust to share your secrets, fears, heartaches and needs with? It would not be wise to do this with any of the regular run of ordinary convicts. They were neither available nor interested. They had their own problems, and to show vulnerability was to open yourself to exploitation.

Many people have two sides. There's the hardened battle-scarred outside – the crusty bit, full of bravado and daring, spoiling for a fight or planning to escape and be a hero. This is the guy you meet when you first enter prison. This is the guy people think populates the prison system. He fits. He lives up to the stereotype. He's the hard and worldly criminal who lacks respect; the leader, the initiator of evil crimes and desperate acts of larceny and violence. A loner, he needs the company and support of no one and is powerful in his chosen craft.

Then there's the other side. It's the side he hides from onlookers and inquirers. He is disinclined to reveal it. This side is his awareness of his madness, his illiteracy, his inner emptiness, his need for love, his low self-image, and his shame for his family and origins. This is the side of him that feeds crumbs through the bars to sparrows when he's on bread-and-water for fifteen days. He understands about homelessness and single parenthood and family oppression, because it's what he has lived with since for ever. He understands about illiteracy and innumeracy, because none of his friends can read and write, and neither can he. It feels unjust. But what can he do? It feels as though someone has failed him who ought not to have done, but who? He has no way of knowing. What he must do is to be more uncaring, more violent, more of a thief, than any of the others. That way, he gains the respect he would have had if he could read and write.

The self-doubting, vulnerable side of this criminal is kept mostly locked away, and that's why no one really knows him as he really is.

On 14 November 1959, in the small village of Holcomb, Kansas, wealthy farmer Herbert Clutter, his wife Bonnie and their teenage son and daughter Kenyon and Nancy were shot and killed in their home. The two young men who committed the crime were Dick Hickock and Perry Smith. They were hanged for it in 1965, just a year ago. He had read all about it in the papers. A fellow prisoner who had worked at the Clutters' farm had told Dick that this would be an easy job of robbery with big money there for the taking. As it happened, it didn't work out that way. Mr Clutter didn't have a safe on the premises (he did all his transactions by cheque and carried very little cash on his person). Dick and Perry got away with a portable radio and about forty dollars. It could just as easily have been Roy and Derek, had there been a gun culture in England as there had been in Kansas.

Four gunshots, and eventually six lives were ended. More than anything else, this left the skinny captive with a sense of wasted lives, the killers' as well as their victims', and that was something the gallows did not put right. The reason the young men's actions in murdering the Kansas farm family appeared senseless was because no one understood their social, emotional, and psychological landscape. They did not know or understand the real, true, essential nature of these two young men, which was their weakness, emptiness, vulnerability and thirst for acceptance. No one knew their 'other side'.

Similarly, few people truly understood the inner landscape or social wilderness of this skinny captive. Someone like the writer Truman Capote, who subsequently wrote a novel about the brothers' story, might. Most would not.

The skinny prisoner felt like that about himself. He remembered what a relief it had been when he discovered that other prisoners cried when they were alone in their cell, just like him. He was glad when he discovered other cons were lost and anxious, just like him. It gave him tremendous strength and encouragement. He never dreamed that the hard and ruthless convict, living a few doors along the gantry, actually cried himself to sleep every night, and that he hid his face in the pillow to muffle the sound. It might say a lot in his favour, since it demonstrated some humanity.

The guards too. They were not hard and heartless. They felt things, just like the prisoners. They cried sometimes when they thought about all those wasted lives. Why else did some of them occasionally show kindness and compassion? They understood all right. After all, they had a living to earn.

He had been told by one of the governors that he is on the verge of tears when he recalls the incident of an old prisoner who did not want to be released because he had nowhere to go and no friends except those in the prison. Sending him on release had been tantamount to a death sentence. He was dead in a month through living as a vagrant on the streets of Luton. It used to amaze the skinny prisoner how people could be so hard on the outside when inside their shell they were so soft and vulnerable.

He had mixed feelings, this much was clear. Whilst objecting to being sentenced without recourse to the legal process, yet he was still philosophical about the generosity of his sentence. Three days incarceration on a bread and water diet. It wasn't much for escaping from prison and stealing three cars and endangering the lives of the police and members of the public. Had two escaping borstal boys not committed it, but two members of the criminal public, it would have carried a considerable sentence in an ordinary court. The Board of Visitors must have sensed how wrecked these two captives were by their experience that they decided to go easy on them.

It was sad, really. Ordinary people, like convicts and prison guards, being kind. It used to confuse him, and he couldn't understand why all this love had to be cloaked by a mock hatred. It was the system that demanded it, not the people themselves. It took him another two months in Wormwood Scrubbs to realise that. He knew, from then on, that he hadn't wasted his time. He was a learner, and he valued what he learned as though it were precious gold. He had begun to discover something about people; something dynamic and real, powerful and promising. It was a long time before he realised exactly what it all meant, but when he did, it was a revelation and a valuable new tool in his people-kit.

After the two months had ended, he was called in from his lonesome walk in the exercise yard – from the time of his return to prison, he had been branded an escapee and clothed in the special uniform, called 'patches' that depicted him as such, and allowed to exercise away from other prisoners, on his own in the company of a guard. Armed guards escorted escapees everywhere they went.

'How do you feel? Asked the Governor.

'I feel OK, Sir.' He replied.

' It has been decided, after due consideration of all the facts, that you will be returned to Gains Hall. The Commissioners thought that you should be given another chance. I hope you won't let them down. You must realise this. It means that if you betray their trust, next time they will come down on you much harder than they have this time. They're sticking their necks out for you. I'd advise you not to let them down.'

The skinny prisoner had his own thoughts. He had not asked for their trust, and so, since it had been imposed upon him without his consent he could not betray it. That was their world. This was his. He did not request soft treatment; they had been that way by their own choice. To respond to trust, you have to be trusted. What they were doing was sending him to borstal. He did not feel that he deserved borstal in the first place, so where did this 'trust' rubbish come from?

He was in his own hopeless intellectual world without the knowledge that his thoughts were accurate, insightful and true. He believed at that time that these thoughts of his were wrong, the preoccupation of a criminal intellect, and therefore not right. He did not know that in years to come they would be vindicated and find proper expression through the exercise of his chosen vocation. His guards and captors could not know this any more than he, of course. The dominant world-view was the criminal justice one, and that prevalent view provided the touchstone of all argument that took place in his prison and at this time in his life.

He knew he would escape again. He did not like this experience that recalled so much of his schooldays, of being treated like a naughty schoolboy. Much as he wished they had not decided to send him back to an open borstal – he would much preferred to go to a closed prison – the deal was done. He had not been consulted about it. He had simply been told. If they had asked him, he would have told them. As it was, he heard what the governor said and then let it go.

Back in the cell, he cried all night. He knew the same process of the past two months was going to be repeated, only next time worse. He knew he would be out of there as soon as the van doors opened.

He spent another two weeks at the Scrubbs. He said nothing. His daily round was silent and resentful. He avoided speaking to anyone whenever possible. It was not difficult, being locked in the cell alone for twenty-three out of every twenty-four hours. He did nothing, or as little as possible. He sat almost catatonic in his cell, breathing shallowly and sleeping much.

The guard came on the appointed day. The captive took his bits and pieces with him. He collected his plastic use-it-for-everything shaving and eating bowl and his toothbrush. He stripped, had a bath, got dressed in stiff prison underwear, got into the van, ignored the weather, and waited for the journey to end. And it happened. Just as he knew it would. Nothing had changed, except that he had been punished and condescended to. His urge for freedom welled-up inside his soul and it was sweet like poison. He knew that the freedom he would gain would be empty, but what else was there to attaint to? That beautiful killer was present in his spirit. Derek was beside him. He had received the same disposal. They glanced coldly at one another. Derek nodded. It was on again.

They did not escape the moment he van door opened. They spent ten days at the open borstal the second time. They had been under observation. On the tenth night, off they went, across the fields, down the road and far away to Bristol at the other end of the country. The weather was foul. Wet, cold and with a cutting wind. Life was not at all pleasurable. They slept in barns, fields and store doorways, and lived on raw potatoes and sprouts from the fields. One morning at three o'clock, sleeping in cardboard boxes in the shop front of a posh store, they were washed away by a jet of water from a hosepipe. It was the local town centre managements' 'clearing-away-of-the-vagrants' hour.

Most of the time the two children wandered until they were lost. Lacking an aim or anywhere to live, and without any street credibility or local knowledge, just as they had gained their freedom, they realised they were in another prison. It was a prison of their own making, though it had no bars, and there was no prison cell. Freedom had curdled and gone sour. For a week, they waited to get caught, but no one came for them.

They were children alone in a big city whose streets were concrete and cold.

Hungry, soaked to the skin, footsore and weary, they wandered into a village along a country road. Had the weather been better, things might have been different. The hunger-pangs gave the illusion of walking two feet above the ground, creating a feeling of intoxication and light-headedness. They felt disoriented and were close to fainting. The village, friendly and intimately scattered around a central grassy knoll, with little pink-washed cottages and bright green lawns, echoed their longings for security, comfort and love. The two free lads sat on the green verge at the edge of the road with their heads in their hands. There was no love here. These were merely private houses, private families, and exclusive groups of individual people.

There was nothing for the likes of them in a place like this. They had run out of tobacco. Sighing heavily, Derek said,

'I've had it. What about you?'

Their fight had gone. Their energy was drained. They had been defeated again, as the skinny escapee had already known.

'There's a police station just down the road.' He said.

'Yeah.' Said Derek.

'What about it? We'll get a meal...'

'Let's go.' He replied.

They approached the front door and pressed the bell; introduced themselves as two escaped borstal boys and went in. The sergeant's wife telephoned her husband and while they waited for him to come home, just like the woman in the previous episode, she cooked them a meal.

He thought of a story he had read in the Bible about a guy who was so hungry he sold his inheritance for a bowl of soup. Whether he had believed the story when he read it at the time, he now knew it was possible. It was quite likely someone would give away his freedom for a meal. Cynically he thought that as it was, freedom wasn't worth a meal anyway, so he'd got the better end of the deal.

The policeman entered the kitchen. He and his wife were friendly and talkative. He made a telephone call, and the two lads braced themselves for whatever revenge the now angry and frustrated Commissioners at the Scrubs would take. Whatever it was, it would be much worse than before. To their minds, they had 'betrayed their trust'. And as was said earlier, they had a particular view about that, which was not the same as the view of the skinny prisoner.

Remembering what the governor had said, they were troubled at the thought of their return. There was every chance that they would be sent to Detention Centre for some real punishment. Reading Detention Centre was the place every convict thought of with dread in his guts. Like they say with the Royal Marines, ninety-nine-percent need not apply. These two escapees did not want to be included in the prison system's equivalent of the Marines' glasshouse. They did not want to be part of the one percent. It was rumoured that reading Detention Centre was hell on earth. The Commissioners were reluctant to send prisoners there, especially obese, diabetic, mentally ill or physically small prisoners. On the other hand, other convicts in the extended English prison system treated people who had been through Reading with the utmost respect.

The skinny prisoner, whatever fears he may occasionally have had, thought that he had already been saved from whatever abuse would be hurled his way. He had given up hope and adopted cynicism as his approach to everything in life. He had ceased caring since it hurt so much.

If he had not set his mind in this way, he would have become a quivering wreck, for he was no hero, nor very brave. A recurring part of his speech had become the phrase, 'Who cares?' It was not a question, but a spat statement of fact. No one cared, least of all him.

He had provided himself with an emotional shock absorber. He would have been as unmoved if the Board of Visitors had sentenced him to death.

Later that day a vehicle arrived outside the village police station and three policemen got out. They went in to the house and shared a cup of tea with the sergeant, his wife and the two who had surrendered themselves. Neither lad knew any of them, which was odd, because they knew every guard on their wing at the Scrubbs. After a friendly chat and the cup of tea, the three got up, and led their captives to the waiting car. It was to be a short drive – much shorter than the drive to London, and in the opposite direction.

'Where are we going?' Asked Derek.

'Gloucester Prison.' Came the terse reply.

'What's it like?'

'A prison.'

It did not look like a prison. Prison was tall, forbidding and grey, with great bars across the windows and pallid faces staring into the void. This was a small red brick structure. Although parts of it were two hundred years old, the front had the appearance of a modern, architectured structure, completely unlike the Scrubbs. Instead of a high eighty-foot blank exterior wall, it had an extensive entrance hall built into the front, and a third of the way up the wall, a long row of ordinary toughened glass green-tinted windows that reflected the blue of the sky ran along two thirds of the building. There was no razor wire to be seen, and two patches of garden, opening to the public street, enclosed in low sandstone walls, lovingly tended, sprouted palm and bamboo greenery. Flowering blooms lay at the foot of a flight of wide grey Portland stone steps leading to the front office. Standing square in full view of stores and public streets, it could have been just another one of the blocks of offices.

Behind the façade was another story of course. A Category 'B' local facility, the certified normal capacity for the establishment being 236, it had an operational capacity of 330. That meant it was overcrowded. In other words, many of the inmates had to share their cell with another. The cells had been built for single occupancy.

Although the prison was on an inner city site, perhaps because of the gardens at its entrance it appeared to the two boys to be surrounded by open country. It was a strange illusion. The prison was however filled mainly with country yokel prisoners with Southwestern accents. There were many young people with clear psychiatric and emotional problems.

Sometimes it felt to him like a psychiatric hospital. The prison catered for the administrative court area that included Gloucestershire, Herefordshire, South Worcestershire, and parts of Avon and Somerset.

A report later to be published about the young prisoners in Gloucester Prison was to highlight the concerns of the staff themselves about their perilous mental and emotional health...

' We continue (as we have mentioned in previous reports) to be extremely concerned about individuals being held at the Prison who have psychiatric or personality disorders. We urge that these individuals be transferred to secure hospital facilities in order for them to receive appropriate specialist care and treatment. We have also noted that there appears to be an excessive amount of time taken for individuals to be transferred to suitable establishments at the present time.'

Here was the most blatant and clear statement and admission of a scandalous situation. This prison whose intention was punishment, not medical treatment, was incarcerating mentally ill people. How many of these people were needing chemical treatment, counselling, surgery, psychotherapy, social interaction and the rest? What were they actually getting? According to the prison officers themselves - who were not employed for their compassionate natures - accustomed to guarding young people and incarcerating them in these stinking tiny cells, depriving them of social interaction and sexual contact as well as of their freedom, this was wrong and ought not to be happening. One may imagine how it felt to the skinny prisoner and others who were not prison guards but their victims.

'Is this it, then?'

'Yes. This is the place.'

The electric gates swung open and a guard peeked out. Waving the vehicle through to the courtyard, he closed the gates behind it. The consignees got out of the car and their escorts unlocked the cuffs, asking without irony whether they had hurt the boys' wrists. They looked at their wrists and said, 'No'. As they strolled in a friendly group towards the Reception block, they chatted in the warm sunshine. The two captives were confused by all of this. They had expected to be roughly treated and punished for their recent escapades. They had yet to understand how the system works. Despite the overcrowding and the preponderance of mentally ill convicts, Gloucester Prison had a compassionate Governor and some kindly officers.

It was the rule of the Governor that determined the ethos of the institution. Good Governor, compassionate prison. Rubbish Governor, rubbish prison. It might not be fair, but it was the way it worked. Many good governors found themselves having to deal with unpalatable political realities – like having to be an unofficial psychiatric unit - such as in this case.

For the two lads, this was to become a place of refreshment and putting on weight, of good food and regular exercise and good relationships. For him, if the sentence had ended at Gloucester Prison under that regime, he would have come to heel as an ex-offender much sooner than he did. It was not, however, to be. There was a lot more to be learned yet, and there was a crucial meeting that had not yet taken place.

The reception officer waved them towards some piles of clothing.

'We should have something here.' He said, as he rummaged through a heap of shirts. He instructed his Trustee to fit the two lads up.

An escapee has to wear a special kind of clothing, which was different from the ordinary convict. It marks him out as someone who is likely to be volatile and to attempt escape. The uniform of such a man consists of a battledress navy blue jacket with a large bright patch – usually Day-Glo yellow or blue, bordered with white – sewn on the left breast. The trousers are the usual grey flannels but with a wide bright yellow or blue patch running down the whole length of the leg. The other leg had a narrower yellow or blue stripe (opposite, depending on the colour of the other stripe). Whatever colours are used, they have to be bright and noticeable. Every escapee has this distinctive uniform. If he escapes, civilians will have their suspicions aroused by this oddly dressed individual, but the main purpose was to immediately distinguish them from other prisoners in the prison. It tells the guards, at a glance, that this is an escapee. A prisoner in this uniform is described as being 'in patches'. He has a constant escort, especially on transfers from one institution to another. He is even escorted to and from the lavatory.

Given this constant surveillance, his stay in Gloucester Prison was not totally unbearable. His experience of the officers was that they were generous and kind. His cell was fitted, as that of an escapee, with a red bulb that was never switched off. He was fast getting used to sleeping in that red glow. It stopped bothering him after a short time. He was kept locked up twenty-three hours a day. His food was brought to the door every mealtime and pushed through the half-opened door. Every afternoon he was taken by armed escort on a circular walk round and round the exercise yard for an hour. As he walked with a cigarette, the escort leaned against the wall with his cigarette.

This went on without interruption for two weeks. He had begun to wonder what sort of a place this was. No work. No free association with the other cons. He had spent a whole two weeks in his cell on his own with only the occasional guard to say hello to at meal delivery times. Being a small person, and having always all of his adult life, been nine stone and four pounds, it was in Gloucester Prison that his weight rocketed to ten-and-a-half stone! After two weeks he asked why he was being kept in solitary confinement. The guard did not know why.

He was soon to discover the answer to his question. Mid afternoon one Tuesday an officer asked him if he would be prepared to talk to someone. He said he was ready to see anyone, having had precious little companionship of late.

He was escorted to one of the visiting rooms. He could not imagine who could have come all of this way to see him. He assumed it may have been his parents, but they were poor and angry and would not have spent precious resources on such a trip. He was intrigued. Maybe it was someone from Gains Hall or the Scrubbs. The guard opened the door of the visiting room and waved him to a comfortably upholstered chair. Opposite the chair sat a huge man in a suit. He had never seen him before. He was clearly a police representative of some sort. C.I.D., maybe. After two weeks of talking to no one, he was prepared to talk to anyone.

'Hello, Roy.' He offered his hand in greeting, cheerfully welcoming him to sit down.

'Copper!' He said, declining the offer of fellowship, preferring to relax in the first proper chair he had sat in for months.

' How are you feeling? Cigarette?'

A pack of expensive cigarettes crossed the table and he took one. He had the feeling all this had been planned a long time ago. He had come to soften him up for interrogation. He had waited two weeks in the hope that the prisoner would be ready to talk. And now, there he was, offering friendship and cigarettes and a few minutes of comfort in exchange for a little bit of grassing. The prisoner decided to let his know how he was feeling.

'Bloody lovely, mate. Haven't felt better for months. I've discovered that I am the best company I could ever had, and I'm reading stuff you wouldn't believe. Plato, Aristotle, Spinoza, Locke, Kant, Descartes, Shakespeare, Dickens, Kierkegaard, and Milton to mention but a few. They've got a great library. You could do with a bit of this yourself!'

He managed with some difficulty not to look too taken aback.

'Enjoying it, are you? Oh well, that's good then. Only some blokes go nuts being locked up all the time for weeks on end, poor bastards.'

The last phrase had no doubt been added to convey an expression of some empathy for the poor solitary prisoner. It was cant, and the skinny prisoner knew it. He did not mistake it for sympathy.

' Come off it, mate.' He said. 'That's just what you want. Blokes start going round the twist, like a lot of them in this place, and then you come along and ask for a confession.'

'Confession? Who said anything about a confession?'

Innocent, smiling look on his face, eyes dilated in mock surprise. Eyebrows lifted. He had misjudged the prisoner and was treating him like a fool. The prisoner, though young and inexperienced, wasn't going to have it. He leaned across the table, engaged the officer's eyeballs, placed his fingertips on the polished surface, and said very slowly,

'All right. What do you want to know?'

He felt that if he knew what he was after, he would be better able to avoid telling him. Suspecting what was happening, the police officer's eyes narrowed and hardened into little steely balls. Though his mouth still smiled, his hands had clenched.

'Two weeks ago, I met a police officer and his wife and I would have told them anything. But not you. Not here, either. I like it here. I really do. The food's good, and I've got a cell of my own on the ground floor. No one bothers me. I don't have to get to know any of the cons or nutters in this place. I've got no worries, and I am not going to speed-up my transfer to the Scrubbs and God knows where else after that. While I'm here with what I know and your bosses want you to find out, I'm happy. You can visit me as often as you like.'

There was nothing the policeman could do to him that had not already been done. Once, he used to worry about other peoples' feelings, but he had become cynically hardened against that kind of weakness.

'Believe it or not, I enjoy being locked up on my own. I read and write and I'm getting an education. I've never had time before. I hope it lasts for as long as it can. I'm a very happy bunny, and I'm not bothered if I spend the rest of my sentence here in Gloucester Prison. There's no chance whatsoever that I'll confess to anything or that there is anything I have to confess to.'

The officer did not mind. There was little he could do if he had. He was there, according to prison tradition and rules, at the sufferance of the prisoner he had come to visit. Roy could terminate the interview at any time, just by saying so.

'All right lad, I'm going to put my cards on the table. Now I don't want you spending the rest of your term in solitary confinement. I don't care what you say, it can't be much fun, and I wouldn't wish that on anyone. As for me putting you there, all I can say is that it wasn't my doing..'

'All I need is for you to admit to taking a number of motor vehicles and some clothing. That's all I want, and it's just to clear up the records. I've got books to be cleared, and more important things to do, quite frankly.

It's not as though we didn't know you are guilty. We've spoken to Derek, and he's told us all about it anyway. We do know what harpooned and what you did. But we need a statement signed – clear the books - and there'll be no more trouble. How's that, eh, lad?'

Of course they were guilty. Everyone knew it. He had all the circumstantial evidence he needed. Just a confession and a signed statement and he would be on his way back to borstal, and the sentence would be resumed. After all, the strongest argument to sign the statement was that as long as he refused, he would be spending time in prison that was not being counted towards his borstal sentence.

Three things stopped him. First, he was not a 'grass'. Second, in an odd way he enjoyed the police officer's visits. It was like a friend from the outside world. Not that the friend cared. He also enjoyed the visit because it was a game of wits, and a game in which he felt he had some power. He had something they wanted. It was a new experience for him. Third, putting off the evil day when the fear and dread of going back to the Scrubbs and getting a Detention Centre sentence would be realised. The longer he could make the present situation last, the better.

He smiled at him, told him to prove his allegations, lit up a cigarette and summoned the guard.

'What I've got is time, and plenty of it.' He said as he left the room.

'If you want to talk anytime, tell the Governor and I'll be down. Don't forget, now.'

He did not contact the Governor. He called to see him once again during those three months, but he refused to see him. By the time of his transfer from that comfortable institution he had spent over three months in solitary confinement, and had read through most of the prison library. He had even got hold of a copy of Das Kapital and read all three volumes. What a collection! Poets, philosophers, economists, biographies of all kinds of people, histories and historians, politicians, thrillers, novels, brilliant literature, the lot. Each one bore its own stamp of authenticity, its own worldview, its own insights and learning. They had been impressed with the stamp of an idea. The idea that a human being is intended for something more than what at first appears. Greater than a physical body, a human being is more than the sum of parts. Greater than the body and more than a stack of dinners. Every book – even the pulp fiction thrillers knocked together in a week and sold in a month, was saying something greater about humankind. Writers, he came to understand, were all optimists, whatever it was they wrote, because they believed it was worth taking the trouble to put it on paper – that there would be people to read what they wrote.

Ideas of 'eternity' and 'life after death', and 'life before death' sprung from the mythologies and religious works and histories and biographies and works of fiction. The idea that people can live better than they do, and love better than they do filled the pages. These things frightened him at first, because he thought they were about other people, and not himself.

But he soon came to understand that he was included in 'humankind' and that these aspirations could be his also. Some of the books denied there was a God or an afterlife. Others asserted that there was. But the mere fact that they all, in some way or another addressed the possibility, intrigued and captured his imagination, spurring him on to even further reading. It was ironic and an indication that God might have a sense of humour, that it was to be in Reading Goal, in solitary confinement, awaiting punishment that most of his prison reading was to be done.

He had a battered Bible. Half the pages were missing, because they made great cigarette papers. One day he went on a thieving trip around the cells until he found a Bible that was complete. Taking it back to his cell, he spent a whole week reading from cover to cover, missing some of the boring bits. He discovered some beautiful stuff there, and some shocking stuff, too. One thing that surprised him was how many of the Old Testament leaders of the Hebrews, who were God's people, had been adulterers, murderers, and morally reprehensible individuals! Not just Cain, but Abraham, Moses, King David. Yet, there was Jesus – the best man who ever lived, part of the same story. It was full of surprising stuff. He could see why it was called the Book of Books. It was about everything.

The policeman came again two weeks before Roy was transferred to Wormwood Scrubbs. He told him nothing, as usual. He went away. He could have proven his case if he had taken it to court. Clearly he had been told to call it a day. After all it had been three months, and it did not look hopeful for him.

It was a sad day for Roy when he left that prison. Reading Detention and the Scrubbs loomed up ahead, and he had also made friends with some of the guards at Gloucester. Two of them escorted him to the station where he boarded the train in the company of two guards from Wormwood Scrubbs. A special compartment had been labelled, *'Reserved for H. M. Prisons'* on the window for all to see. The compartment fell silent as they neared London.

The Scrubbs officer at the station looked hard at the young man in handcuffs who alighted from the train. He had been separated from his companion Derek. There was no sign of recognition or welcome from the officer. Roy feared that what the future held was pain and suffering of a kind he had never experienced before. He wasn't angry about it, for he had known it was coming, and he had nothing to measure it against. The only way it *could* happen was like this. He smiled at the officer and a tear of regret and self-pity ran down his cheek. Did the officer smile for a nanosecond, and then the mask slide back over his eyes as though such a moment of compassion had never occurred? The skinny prisoner couldn't say.

This was not going to be like Gloucester Prison.

Study

People loved Jesus for His miracles, and He received their praise. However, he wept over Jerusalem because He knew how fickle peoples' hearts were, and how quickly they change their minds. Do you know that God loves you even when you're inconsistent in how you feel about Him? It's true.

Pray

for individuals being held in our prisons who have psychiatric or personality disorders. Urge God to move those with authority to transfer these individuals to hospital facilities in order for them to receive appropriate specialist care and treatment. Pray for there to be a shorter time taken for individuals to be transferred to suitable establishments. Pray for healing rather than retribution.

READING GOAL

The officer went to his cell in the Scrubs and led the skinny prisoner to the room where the Commissioners waited to pass sentence. By this time, after a few weeks of the Scrubs routine, the old fears had been socialised back into him. He had become less confident as the day drew nearer. Those easy months of weight-gain and education in Gloucester had softened him. He'd allowed thoughts of love, mercy, goodness, justice and fair play to get a hold on him. He had secretly hoped he would get a soft sentence; that they would question him about his new philosophy of life and detect the change in his attitude. Maybe he would get six days bread and water and a return to Gains Hall. If so, he would settle down to the rest of his term and behave.

With these thoughts in his mind, plus a dread of the unknown horrors that might wait in Reading Detention Centre, he approached the panelled door and entered the Commissioners' room.

Half a dozen people sat around a highly polished table. He knew from the aura of the group that the sentence was going to be a punishing one. He could read their faces. Determination, pity and revenge.

The saga of his former crimes, including the most recent, was read out to him. He had not realised there had been so many. More than fifty, in fact. He had been a bad lad, but it was only him who knew it was a long scream for understanding and for help. In those days, no one understood this, as they say they do now. He had seen a painting by Francis Bacon that depicted exactly how he felt, as though internal pressures were blowing off his head. A persistent criminal was a persistent criminal, and the punishment of the criminal should fit the criminal's crime. That was fair, wasn't it?

Well, no. It might be a good line in a comical musical, or headline in a tabloid, but not a good guide for criminal justice. However, you can't know what you don't know, and these people didn't know what was happening in the skinny prisoner's heart and mind.

He was berated with the reminder of their previous kindness and generosity, and how they had forgiven his betrayal of their trust. Yet he had consistently rejected them. He was no longer to be trusted. He must learn that the disposals of the Commissioners must be obeyed. He was accused of treachery, betrayal of trust, and a general lack of honesty and dependability.

He was in no mood or position to argue, and his silence was taken as insubordination and a refusal to repent. One of the Commissioners informed him that he was sentenced to spend fifteen days in solitary confinement in the block on bread and water. Three days on and three days off meant that he would have at least another month in the Scrubbs before where he was to be sent from there. He reeled at the size of the disposal. Fifteen days was a whole month in 'chokey'.

That was a long time. He thought of 'The Great Escape'.

Before he could recover from the blow this had dealt him, the voice of the leading Commissioner pierced his skull,

'You are also to be consigned to Reading Detention Centre for a period of punishment for not less than three months.' Silence. A female fly buzzed against the windowpane. The universe was empty.

Sitting on the floor – there was no chair - in the isolation 'chokey' cell, dazed, it was at least half an hour before he was able to seriously address his sentence with any amount of mental clarity. He crossed his legs and rocked from side to side for an eternity. He made no sound – just a gentle humming to reassure himself. Thus he sat for hours, swaying gently from side to side.

For the length of the bread and water punishment he communicated with no one. He was not allowed any reading material apart from a Bible, which he read little of during that time. He grabbed the bread when it came and saved none for the birds. They could go and scavenge somewhere else. He spent hours of his time quoting Shakespearean soliloquies from memory. He had made them a part of his own psychological experience. They expressed exactly what was in his heart and mind. They anchored him in his humanity and saved his sanity. He thought of God occasionally and cursed Him for his modesty in refusing to reveal Himself. He learned to mimic lots of famous people, and would set up and hold conversations and debates between them. The things he made the Queen say to Harold Wilson would not bear repeating. He undid the murder of Caesar, and had him in a gay role in relation to Brutus, and instead of ugly murder, it became a tiff over who had what for breakfast.

He found a bit of matchstick that had been burned and started to draw a bust of a beautiful woman on the glossed back wall of the cell. Although the guard couldn't have avoided seeing it, they took no action to have it removed. They said nothing. One of the Kitchen Trustees kept him supplied with pencils and a bit of sandpaper through the broken eye of the door. He spent many days on that picture, drawing, erasing, smudging, and re-drawing until it seemed to spring to life off the wall. The proportions and shades had to be exact and true to life. He couldn't be satisfied. He had become totally engrossed in the drawing so that when his bread and water arrives, it was an intrusion into his activity. Eventually it was done. He felt that whatever way he looked at the picture it was perfect. It completely satisfied him. There was not a line or shade or highlight out of place. The image was lifelike. It stood out from the wall, giving life and human femininity to the whole dead room.

One day a guard intruded into the privacy of the bread and water skinny prisoner's room. He ordered him to wipe the picture off the wall. To the guard, it was a picture. Who could tell the whole long story of what it was to the prisoner? Whose job was it to explain? The letter of the law required the removal of the illegal scrawling, but the spirit of hope required it's immortalising.

'Take that effing scribble off the wall!'

The effing scribble came off the wall, as the guard had commanded. Its effing impression remained in the heart of the skinny prisoner however, and it remains today.

The Day came for transfer to the Detention Centre all too soon. Among the rest of the victims, chosen for this special period of torture, he got in to the vehicle. It was a transit-type van, with a row of seats on either side fitted with handcuff stations especially by the security service. These, of all borstal boys, had been chosen for the esteemed honour and special victimisation of being selected for a term of punishment in reading Goal.

They lit their cigarettes and recounted jokes and stories they had heard thus far in the prisons. They displayed all the expectations of enjoying the journey and ribbing the guards about their truncheons in comparison with the size and firmness of other things in their possession. This group of secretly terrified prisoners appeared to consider themselves old hands at the business. If one were to ask, 'the business of what?' One might answer, 'The business, this time, of being victims.'

The building, like Gloucester Prison, was made of red brick. Its perimeter wall rose eighty feet above the pavement. There was no razor wire on the summit. Beyond that wall rose another, red brick with a line of white bricks along the top, just below the rim of the building. In the centre of the inner block rose a tower. Red brick again, castellated, a mixture of Georgian and Victorian styles, with two large stacks of Victorian chimneys. The cell windows were picked-out in white against the red brick, and the whole building was square and squat surrounded by its car park. Above the wall few cell windows were revealed to the outside world. It presented as a private place.

Indeed, what went on there was mostly a shame and a disgrace, which the outside world either did not care or did not want to know about. These prisoners, however, were soon to be initiated into the whole enchilada of a sadistic regime that persisted at that time. They were to soon realise that they had now become the victims of it. Probably, in their defence, the Sentencing Commissioners at Wormwood Scrubbs had no idea of the detailed truth of events that regularly occurred against immature boys and psychiatrically sick children and "Tom o' bedlams" in this place of shame. That it was, at least partly, staffed by predatory sadists and abusers.

The officers that accompanied the prisoners from the Scrubbs were sent down from reading. They seemed friendly enough for most of the journey, joking with the prisoners and taking some insults, harmlessly intended, from them.

The group of prisoners, unaware that they were in fact now caught without redemption in the victim net, had begun to feel quite at home and brave after their initial reserve. In fact, the skinny prisoner was beginning to wonder why everybody had made such a fuss about reading Goal. Perhaps, he thought, it was a hangover from the myths about a former famous prisoner, Oscar Wilde. He had written a heart-wrenching poem about the demonic and heartless lack of a compassionate nature in this place. The myth had obviously gotten out of hand...

With no introduction and without warning the heavy blade of the guillotine, balanced for the first few miles of the journey in its unseen cradle above them, sliced into the block of their complacency. 'Chooonk!'

'Right, you lot of slimy worms, get your effing boots, belts, ties and braces off! I want them on the effing floor. Socks, trousers, ties. Ten seconds, and if they're not on the floor by then, you will be.'

After ten seconds and one of the prisoners had not managed to quite comply – he had forgotten to remove his tie – the promise was unequivocally kept, because the officer kicked him hard in the groin and tore the tie from his bruised and reddened neck. He was, as had been promised, on the floor.

'We do not mess about at Reading.' He calmly pointed out, which already had become quite clear.

The prisoners had magically become totally subservient. In the ordinary world some of them would have fought back. But this was a power and politics and psychology game, in which the guards held all the cards. The prisoner – like the slave of old – could not win. He was the property of the state - body, mind, and soul. The state gave him birth and the state gave him death.

All power and glory to the state, and to the state's officials all obedience. Amen.

The guard grasped his truncheon, the other guards following suit. He had never seen a truncheon at close quarters before. Heavy and dangerous. He dared not study it too closely, though it fascinated him. He just did as he was told, double-quick time. They were approaching the gate of Reading detention Centre.

'Cigarettes! Here! Now!' He pointed his stick at a precise spot on the floor. All knew that he wanted the stuff right there, on that exact and precise spot. Not to the left. Not to the right, but there!

'You won't be leaving this place the way you arrived.' He announced. At that time, none of them knew what he might have meant. Certainly, few would have understood some of the subtler psychological and cultural transformations that this regime would force upon them. The transit van braked at the interior gatehouse, and they were kicked unceremoniously out.

'Line up! Five seconds! They formed themselves into a single line, side by side, facing forward.

'Right. Get down them stairs, across the nick and line up in the corridor. Get moving!'

No one knew where 'the corridor' was, having only then arrived. Like the Gadarene herd they followed the victim in front, headlong through the courtyard in the general direction of the guard's pointed finger. It happened that he was heading in the wrong direction. The guard hit him across the head and he ran in another direction. The rest followed him, and the intelligent ones decided that here in Reading punishment prison, you did not take the lead. If you did, you would be punished. They did not reward leadership here. They took it to be rebellion.

Eventually, after a long sadistic ritual that led the little group around most of the courtyard, they discovered the 'corridor' and shuffled into a line against the wall.

A nasty little guard with a piggy face and empty metallic eyes waddled to the front of the group and strutted along the row. He was small of stature but with a big gut. His nose was crooked as though someone had slammed a cell door against it.

He swore for five minutes, his face reddening as he tore through the script of his angry soliloquy. He had done this before. It was politic to stand and listen and not move.

One of the lads had a moist nose and had to keep sniffing. He happened to give a particularly hard sniff that coincided with a silence in the guard's rant. He decided to take this as an insubordination. Tightening his fist into a hard little ball, very slowly and deliberately, he rammed it right into the prisoner's face. There was a squelch and a crack. The prisoner tottered backwards and regained his balance. The little officer looked at him with a steely intensity, willing the prisoner to sniff again, and annoyed that he hadn't knocked him to the floor.

Apparently intent on having another go, his attention was diverted by another victim, who momentarily shuffled with rage, surprise, or discomfort. The guard set on him, and kneed him hard in the groin. The boy dropped to his knees moaning and clutching himself. The little officer was sweating and grunting with rage. He looked along the line. The skinny prisoner was terrified that he would be noticed – for being skinny or small or for something he hadn't noticed about himself. He stayed as still as he could, standing at attention like the rest of them.

'Empty your pockets.' He ordered.

Nothing but a handkerchief. He had escaped. Then guard had moved along the line.

'Empty your pockets.' He ordered again. A tall, gangling prisoner with a sunken chest. He turned his pockets inside out. A handkerchief. Nothing else. The guard by this time was very angry. He grabbed the lad's pocket and jerked it from its stitching, taking the pocket right off. Ramming the torn pocket into the lad's face, he screamed,

'What's this?'

'Pocket, sir.' Said the new victim.

Crunch! The officer's fist sunk into the lad's abdomen; the lad lurched forward. The guard's knee came up and met his face and as he straightened up in recoil from the blow the officer smashed his head into his face. All the time the guard was shouting and screaming and cursing.

The other officers present witnessed the whole thing from start to finish. They did and said nothing.

'Tobacco!' Screamed the little stubby officer. 'Tobacco!'

In the corner of the stitched pocket was the tiniest trace of Black Shag dust that must have been in that pocket through the laundry a dozen times. The guard, the prisoners now understood, did not really need an excuse, and the strict letter of the law was on his side. You did well to remember this while spending time in this institution.

The skinny victim's stomach tightened throughout the episode, though he did not dare grit his teeth and betray a tightened jaw muscle that might have set the sadist off against him. However, every one of them must have wished to kill the officer. He must have been the most hated man in the prison service.

The command to run to their cells was given. They ran as hard as they could, but no one had told them which cell was theirs. It was a question of trying each empty cell and see if it fits. Each carried a huge bundle of clothing and bedding. A guard prodded and harried each prisoner as they struggled in their crazy quest. Eventually, the skinny victim found a cell and tripped onto his face, sprawled on the floor among the dishevelled clothing.

For a minute, he was disoriented and dazed. Looking up, he saw a friendly-looking prison guard and said without thinking,

'Oh! Hello, Sir.'

He could not think of anything else to say except maybe to fall down and kiss his boots.

The guard rushed towards the little prisoner, fists flailing. He tried to scramble to his feet and tense his stomach muscles and protect his face with his arms, waiting for it to happen.

It did. For about ten minutes.

Then, it was over.

He lay sobbing in a corner of the cell. Another officer popped his head in ten minutes later to see if Guard Johnson had done a good job on him. Johnson appeared at the door, and the skinny prisoner got into a foetal position, waiting for another beating. The guard said,

'Next time this door opens, I want your name and your number, and I want you standing at attention. Even if you're on the lavatory. And you say 'Sir' before and after everything. Got it?'

He said, 'Yes, Sir.'

The officer stood above him, his great black boot touching his face as he lay on the floor.

'That's, "*Sir* Yes Sir!"'

'Sir, Yes Sir.' He replied.

The door slammed shut. They were gone. Blood had soaked down his shirt. He was defeated, locked up and unwanted. He had the strange feeling that his body had been invaded, like a rape, although it wasn't a rape. It was an intimate enforced intrusion. It cut much more deeply than the flesh. It invaded his soul. If the function of institutionalised violence was to defeat the victim's spirit, its function had been achieved in this instance. Knowing where his best chance for survival lay, he quickly surrendered to the Gradgrind mentality of the institution by the voluntary subjugation of imagination and creativity. For many months to come he was to repress these vital aspects of himself. It would be a long time before his spirit returned. When eventually it did, the transformation was to be miraculous and acknowledged by all.

'God!' He prayed, 'If you're there, help me!'

Beatings and deliberate humiliations went on for weeks, never letting-up. The prisoners had to be out of bed by 6.30 in the morning and standing at attention by their beds. Snow or rain, in physical training sports gear, they had to be running round the exercise yard before the days' work, which itself was killing. The first morning, an obese prisoner was finding it hard to get through the exercises. He could not physically jog trot for more than a few strides at the best of times. The little guard caught sight of his next victim struggling to jog as fast as he could round the exercise yard.

Seeing another opportunity for fulfilling his lust for violent sadism against people for whom he had a duty of care, the nasty little officer grabbed the fat boy by the shorts and dragged him around the yard on his bleeding knees. His fat body was battered and torn on the black gravel of the yard.

Sobbing and bleeding he was left in the yard by the lavatory. Out of breath for running, the guard kicked the sobbing body, took up his stick and strutted to his next duty.

The boy did not appear among the new intake prisoners again. None of them knew what had happened to him. One of the other guards said that after that episode the fat boy was put among another group and, quite miraculously, ran like the rest of them. The prisoners had a different myth. They said that he had killed himself. No one could say which was the true account.

Two hours were spent every day in the most gruelling physical exertion. It was nothing to have to spend half an hour hanging upside down on the wall bars on the orders of the instructor. Every time the body quivered with the strain, because the arms were threatening to tear themselves from the sockets, the instructor would shout and bawl to keep them going. Prisoners would hang on, however, because they had seen the alternative, which was a beating, or starting again with a trebling of the amount of time hanging on the bars.

The skinny victim spent every waking hour of his time at the Detention Centre in terror for his life. Word had gone round the prison on a number of occasions that this or that lad had killed himself. Each moment in his cell, he expected something terrible to happen. Every time there was a footfall on the gantry, he froze. His body suffered this level of heightened anxiety, with the concurrent flooding over-production of adrenaline, every day for over three months.

Alongside the two hours physical exercise in the gymnasium, was the daily work. This consisted of two possible occupations.

The first form of work was the sawing of railway sleepers by the use of a two-handled manual band saw. This required one prisoner at each end of the saw. The teeth of the band saw were about half-an-inch deep, and bit into the tar-and bitumen-soaked wood reluctantly as the tool was dragged back and forth for three hours in the morning without stopping, and then another three hours in the afternoon without stopping. The sawn sections had to be six inches long. The sleepers were about nine feet in length, and the requirement was for six sleepers to be sawn in the morning and another six the afternoon.

A victim dressed in black battledress jacket and long grey flannel trousers stood at either end of the saw. The heavy clothing made them perspire, and the sweat dripped off the ends of their noses. The saw swung back and forth, singing merrily in the sunshine with the vibration of steel against hardwood. Neither worker made a sound. They'd fix themselves to the saw, work, and wait for the end of the day to come. The sections fell to the ground in a regular litany as the row of workers swung back and forth, back and forth, back and forth. A guard watched under a canopy shaded from the burning sun. One wrong move or the slightest indication of talking invited an intervention by a guard who meted out a punishment that could be anything or nothing.

From just across the way the sound of thunder rolled out from under the roof of a large wooden hut. Continually. Inside the long, low hut about twenty young lads were chopping the sticky black sections into firewood. Sharp little hatchets flashed up and down almost faster than the eye could see. Each stick of wood measured half an inch by half an inch by six inches. Any deviation from that approximate measurement would be met with dire consequences. These victims, too, had a quota to complete. By the end of the day, most victims were physically exhausted. Cutting and slicing injuries were common, and increased in number as the day went on. It was not unknown for a lad to lose a finger.

If a saw operator cut himself, a chopper would be moved along to take over his handle, and a bundler would be moved to the chopper position. However, the bundles would still have to keep up. The Israelites in Egypt had a similar problem when making bricks with no straw for the Pharaoh. They had Moses representing them, but these victims had no such hero. The saw operator who had cut himself would be back at bundling as soon as his wound had been bandaged. The second form of work was equally exhausting and physically demanding.

This was the knitting of steel wire fencing. The process was housed in a shed containing five large knitting machines that almost reached the ceiling ten feet above. Each machine had a long metal handle-crank at one end. A prisoner would crank this large handle very slowly, causing a pulley to thread a long wire forward through the machine. A system of cogs in the machine caused the wire to bend at regular intervals of two and a half inches and curl over, threading itself through the previous length of wire that had been through the same process. As each length of wire was fed through the machine, a prisoner would snip the end and tie it around the previous wire-end in a single deft twist with a pair of pliers.

The result was the creation of the wire fencing that can be seen along a million gardens and establishments throughout the world. This fencing operation was as physically demanding, and even more mentally and psychologically stultifying, than the railway sleeper sawing. It was the job no one wanted, especially on the days when someone on the outside had ordered a thicker-gauge, or a green plastic-covered fence, to be knitted.

Although in the whole of the prison there was not a single cigarette to be seen, and no drugs, now and then you would smell a whiff of cigarette smoke along the gantry. However this would not be a prisoner. It would be a bored guard, grabbing a puff whilst the Chief Officer was occupied on something else. If a prisoner were ever to be caught with a cigarette, the lads guessed, he would be in for worse than hell. For the whole of his time at reading Detention Centre the skinny victim had only three drags on a cigarette.

No one ever thought of escape from Reading Prison unless it was through suicide. Escape was impossible on every level, including psychologically. There is a point at which a humiliated and downtrodden victim thinks of himself as rightly and justly a slave, and accepts his position. Welcomes it, even, as a relief from the struggle. When this happens, the thought of escape or any aspiration for something better becomes a blasphemy against what is right and true. Talking was not allowed anywhere in the prison. it was like the Roman Catholic monastery at Mount St Bernard, in which the unspeaking monks glide silently by, hardly disturbing the air in the chapel. Each prisoner was entirely isolated and alone. Indeed, the only two way out of the system were suicide or psychological repression.

Occasionally a prisoner would try to get out by faking a suicide attempt. They knew that the Home Office authorities got politically embarrassed over suicide rates in prisons. They reasoned that the authorities would want to remove from the system any individuals who showed a tendency to suicide, especially in a stressful situation such as at reading Detention Centre. The last thing they wanted was a spotlight on the regime at Reading.

Fake suicides could be accomplished by swallowing a razorblade bound with a good layer of Sellotape to afford protection. On the X-Ray the blade would show but the Sellotape not. Unfortunately, this was an old trick and the guards and staff in the Medical Wing were wise to it. They would simply give the lad a kicking, fail to record it as an attempt at suicide, put the offender in the Block and wait for him to pass the blade. When that happened, the victim would be given another kicking and returned to his cell.

During his time there, the skinny prisoner's neighbour swallowed a needle for real. He was serious to get out of the hell of Reading Goal, the Bedlam. It is a terrible thing for same people to have mad people as their gaolers, and that was what it was.

The only good thing about the goal was the food. There was plenty of it, and it was excellent. Even better than the food at Gloucester Prison. If the food had been bad, not many of the victims would have survived their three months sentence.

After two months of exercises in the gymnasium, sawing and chopping, and turning the fence-handle in the wire shop, he had a body like a little greyhound. Every muscle shone and gleamed, every twist of hard flesh stood against the skin, straining to burst, like little piles of rocks, his arms, legs, abdomen and shoulders shone. He could run for hours with no effort and was never tired. When ruminating in his books, every word went in and his memory had improved beyond anything he had experienced before. He felt that he was newly alive. The previously hated physical exercise had become great fun and relaxation, and the cold showers every session, ironically made life into a luxury. After three months he had bowed to the system and accepted it. He was fit in every part of his body. He no longer feared any beatings, which no longer hurt, and every mealtime there was that fantastic food.

He often looked through his cell window during those last days. He could see the river and a park, and didn't mind that he couldn't go out and enjoy it. In his cell he was safe. He didn't really want to go to another borstal after that. He would much preferred to stay where he was.

So after thirteen weeks the day came for him to leave. He was kicked into the van, which didn't bother him. He said goodbye to the sadists, and started his journey to Rochester Borstal. He had been told that Rochester was where he would complete his sentence. The borstal differed from Gains Hall in that a wall surrounded it. It was both good and bad to leave reading behind. He never got to love the guards, but he had come to enjoy the routine, and the security provided by the discipline.

When he had gone through the periods of being locked away all alone he had made the best of it. He had found it enjoyable and even useful. Like in Gloucester Prison. When he had undergone the hell of Reading Detention centre he had made the best of that. Both had been terrible experiences in the different ways. Yet he had been able to assimilate and overcome them, adding them to his bag of experience.

It seemed wonderful to him that the human personality could suffer all kinds of humiliations and shocks, such devastating blows, and yet become reconciled to them and come out smiling. A human being has such reserves of physical and mental power. He remembered that prayer he had prayed in his cell when the chips were down and he had become defeated,

'God, if you're there, help me.'

He reflected – maybe he *was* there, and maybe he *had* helped him.

Study

Luke 22: 63 to 23: 25. Jesus faced jeering, bullying, accusation and hatred without calling on heaven to rescue Him and wipe out His accusers. He understood what was going on and why He had to die. How sure are you that you are in the right place doing the right things? Ask God for His guidance today.

Pray

Bring before God the pleas of those who are suffering unjustly and secretly at the hands of sadistic government officials.

ROCHESTER BORSTAL

By the time he got to Rochester he had lost all taste for escape. He just wanted to finish his time and leave. It would happen more quickly if he behaved himself and obeyed the rules. He had become quite convinced that the little man was no match for the huge and complex police and prison system. This was Rochester. He had decided that this would be his settling-down place. He had been through his rebellion.

An official report on the prison described it as 'a disgrace' and warned some of its practices could be illegal.   Chief Inspector of Prisons Sir David Ramsbotham had said that Rochester Prison was guilty of *'institutional neglect'*, and particularly criticised the treatment of illegal immigrants and young offenders.

He said that *'the young offenders' wing, in what had been Britain's first Borstal, was filthy and infested with vermin.'* Roy was to discover the truth of this. He was to be locked in a large wicker basket in the prison laundry as a prank by other prisoners, and to find to his horror that the room was crawling with cockroaches.

Sir David's report said that nearly seventy prisoners aged seventeen to twenty-one years were living in a wing that was *'filthy, vandalised, infested with vermin and subjected to an impoverished regime in which the only constant was its unpredictability.'*

This was the place to which Roy, who had already completed seventeen months of incarceration, but had not yet started his borstal sentence, had finally been consigned.   Far from ideal, it was nevertheless to become for him a moment of destiny.

When he arrived therefore at the gatehouse of Rochester Prison he was, as far as legally was concerned, a 'new boy', just beginning his borstal sentence. He was treated as a new boy by the guards. He was taken through all the reception preliminaries, like having a medical, getting personal details recorded and listing any personal property. This had all been done many times before in each of the six prisons and borstals he had been to. He was an old hand at it, and knew the patter of the officers as they ran through the rules and regulations for his intake group:

Guard: *'Wallet, one. Money, none. Watch, none. One large, nearly white, handkerchief. O.K., lad that's you. Next!'*

Prisoner: *Sir!*

Guard: *'Religion?'*

Prisoner: *'Don't know, Sir. Not religious, Sir.'*

Guard: *'Well you're not Jewish. Roman Catholic, C of E, Muslim, Hindu, Buddhist, something else? You must pick one. Unless you're one of them atheists or something...'*

Prisoner: *'None, Sir.'*

Guard (turning to the scribe behind the desk): *'That'll be Church of England, then!'*

Prisoner: *'Yes, Sir.'*

Roy the borstal boy didn't know much about the differences. It didn't bother him and he didn't argue. He believed there might be a God but didn't know exactly which God to have, or what the Gods might be like. He had read about Greeks and Romans, but knew nothing about Allah or the deities of Hinduism. Gods could be nasty as well as nice, and he wasn't really into religion. It was something for posh old ladies. Working class British convicts did not have an interest in church.

One day on the weekly trip to chapel, the single file of lads passed the Roman Catholic chapel where the priest stood at the door. One of the boys dared Roy to say something insulting to him, so he said,

' Good morning, dad.' Thinking that this would be taken as mocking his religion, making him mad. Of course, it did not have that effect at all, and when the priest replied in a kindly and fatherly tone, 'Good morning my son.' It left Roy somewhat confused.

It was in a strange way some kind of a release however. For the past three months he had learned the hard lesson of keeping his mouth shut and not voicing his opinion, or of having a personality. He had been conditioned to shut up. In this case, the elderly Catholic priest had simply returned his greeting and ignored any offence. Roy had laughed and rejoined his compatriots in the chapel queue.

At the front of the borstal chapel there stood a life-sized carving of Jesus hanging and dying on a cross. It was executed in rich brown, almost red mahogany. Jesus on his cross. Many had been the time he had studied that statue. It was full of pain; like Roy had been when as an innocent he had been getting an unjust beating in Reading Goal. There was that about it. A sense of the injustice of Jesus' suffering. Yet is was full of something else; something beautiful – beyond the art of it; something peaceful and resigned, or wise. It fascinated him. He'd often watch it as the preacher did his stuff in the pulpit, or the priest intoned his words at the Communion table. Off he would go into his own world, through that carving, all alone, watching the wooden face. He must have known what it was to suffer. He wondered why they did it to him, being as he was innocent and that everyone knew it.

On the other hand Jesus had been like him, a criminal. Just like the rest of the people in Rochester Prison. So he was in the right place. He remembered reading in Gloucester Prison how the police of his day had Got Jesus for causing a riot. Riotous behaviour was not an insignificant crime.

Anyway, the story went that the police were scared of him because he had the people on his side. It was only the authorities that were threatened by him. The people thought he was great. In the end they took the easy way out and fitted him up on a trumped up charge. Having no-where like Rochester to send him to, they finished him off. He was only one among many other rebels of his day, and no one would remember it in a week. They hadn't reckoned with the fact that a week is not a long time in religion, and religious people have very long memories.

Crucifixion was the authorities' way of sorting out criminals. Roy thanked God he had been born in the Twentieth Century.

There was something about that statue that wasn't quite right, though. Not for a man who had been strung up as a criminal. Not for someone who had been accused of stirring-up violence and murder. It was something about the face. The person who had carved it could have made his face hard and violent-looking, but he hadn't. He had made it angelic and innocent-looking; other-worldly. Why would he do that?

Over the months, Sunday after Sunday, he began to understand the statue's face, though it remained baffling.

Once a week, two gay men dressed in what the prisoners called 'brown frocks' but that the wearers called 'habits' would visit the prison. They were Franciscan Friars. They were doing some religious course down the road in the village near the prison, training to be priests. In the early days of their visits the lads would mock them, but after a while they became wallpaper and were not noticed. They would bring cigarettes, and take some of the prisoners out for a meal occasionally. All the lads thought that they were gay, but no one ever complained about them. They were friends of the Prison Chaplain, who was after getting as many religious conversions as possible from among the prisoners. Roy was OK with that. After all, it was his job.

The Chaplain was tall and skinny and with large hands. He would visit the prison every Sunday after supper. He never brought cigarettes, but had the same sort of look as the Jesus statue. Roy couldn't figure him out. Why was he there, in a prison, when he could be somewhere else in a wealthy parish drinking sherry with the local lord?

Roy was having a game with some of the lads after lunch in the prison kitchen. There was a lad everyone called 'Chopper'. They were playing with the cutlery whilst doing the washing-up. Chopper grabbed a huge carving knife and started waving it about, and approached Roy in a mock-threatening challenge. Roy jumped away in fun and made a face at Chopper, sticking his tongue out and his head to one side. Chopper continued to advance, knife in hand. The knife flashed in the light as he wielded it above his head and brought it down in a stabbing motion reminiscent of Norman Bates in the Psycho movie that had been doing the cinemas just before Roy's imprisonment. They were only playing. It was a game. But what if he were3 to misjudge one of those lunges? Roy was scared and smiled at Chopper, asking him to put it down now the game was over. But Chopper had not finished. He sensed Roy's apprehension, and this somehow inspired his madness. The knife was sharp and in the wrong hands deadly. Roy made a relaxed move towards the door, signifying that the game was over and there was some clearing-up to be done in the dining room. Chopper did not get the message. The knife was raised again, just above Roy's face, and began to descend with some force. He had done some self-defence as a young man, and by instinct his forearm lifted towards the knife, and his right hand grabbed at Chopper's wrist as the knife came down.

Unluckily, his hand caught the blade of the weapon and he could feel the tendon between his thumb and forefinger gently slice in two.

Well, this had to be explained to the guard somehow. All injuries had to be reported. Were this incident to be reported in a certain way, the man who had two convictions for armed robbery and was now serving a borstal sentence for grievous bodily harm may have seriously intended it as a violent attack. Might a prosecutor assert that it was an attempt to murder another prisoner?

Whatever had been on Chopper's mind, he did have a history of macabre violence. He used to tell the 'funny' story of a rocker who visited his cafe in London. The lad sat at the bar with a lager in his hand, and Chopper, who got his name from his job as a butcher's boy, approached him. He said to the lad,

'I like your parting.' Pointing to the rocker's hairdo.

'Wot parting?' asked the rocker.

'That one!' Said Chopper, bringing a meat cleaver down on the lad's head, splitting his skull in two.

It would not do to make too much of a fuss over the incident in the kitchen. Just be thankful for one small cut. Roy explained the cut to the guard, who took him across to the Medical Officer, who stitched it up with no anaesthetic.

The Chaplain was in the hospital office when he arrived. They fell into conversation and Roy asked the question that had been on his mind for some months about why Jesus was in the prison chapel. They talked for a while, as his hand was being stitched, and Roy accepted his invitation to attend a Bible class.

These went on each week for some months on Friday evenings, and there was nothing else to do, so he attended every one.

Their discussion ranged across the whole breadth of the Christian faith. One of them had been about the Bible as the word of God. The Christianity stands or falls on whether the Bible is true or not. Millions of people, he said, had staked their lives on it. Destiny-making trust had been placed in it, while other people have tried to get rid of it and expunge it from history. Nevertheless, it has gone on and grown stronger, becoming the all-time world best seller. Some nations have based their charters on it. Though it has been the cause of extraordinary good things in the world, other people with hateful motives, have made it the excuse for doing terrible wrongs. No book in history has been so studied and scrutinised, so used, and so abused as the Holy Bible.

Together, they discussed the supernatural nature of the Bible's content. They considered, for example, the miraculous claims such as fulfilled prophecies, and the ultimate assertion of Jesus' divinity and power in his resurrection from the dead. That was something Roy had sensed in his meditations on the wooden statue. He hadn't until then realised that the Bible itself said Jesus was God!

They looked a bit at the literary, archaeological, and historical arguments for the Bible's authenticity, too. This was a bit academic, and Roy had no way of knowing at that time that in the future he would be actually teaching these things to trainee priests in universities...

That is to jump ahead too far, though.

They put him to work in the laundry. He found it great fun, shoving everybody's clothes into an industrial washing machine and watching it go round. It was not a heavy labouring job, and he was able to wear clean clothing for it. One of the fun bits about this machine was when it was overloaded. The tub would spin and wobble, threatening to tear it from its moorings. This would upset the civilian Launderer, employed to train the lads in the job, and who was not a prison guard, but it was a laugh. The laundry lads had new shirt every day, with the largest collars. A large collar in prison was an Alpha Male signal. Ironic, in that there were no females to impress.

There were a number of other jobs in the laundry. The colander machine, like a huge heated mangle on which sheets were ironed, was a warm and cosy job, especially in the cold winter. You could put food particles in it and see what shape and colour stains you could impress on the clean pillowcases and bed linen.

Round the back of the laundry was the drying room, in which large wicker baskets were used to store the dried garments prior to transporting and distributing them to the prison wings. The baskets were placed in front of two huge industrial fan heaters built into the wall. The heat was stifling, just to enter the room. One of the initiation ceremonies for new laundry-lads was to lock them in one of these baskets and leave them for an hour directly in front of the drying fans. It was pure luck that no one, as far as anyone knew, had been killed in this process. The place was crawling with cockroaches, which seemed to love and thrive on the conditions of heat and damp.

Chad joined the group one Tuesday morning. He was tall and thin and had a large tattoo of an eagle across his hairless and sunken chest. When the

Launderer's back was turned, the lads grabbed Chad and stuffed him bodily into the large industrial Bendix washing machine and turned it on. It had been installed on its side, with the viewing window facing to the front, and was about five times the size of a household machine.

His terrified face peered out from behind the toughened transparent plastic. It was very funny, especially when one of the lads pretended to reach for the water-tap. The lad was frightened out of his wits, as he went round and round with the washing.

Joe decided it wasn't funny enough, so he turned the water on. They could dry Chad out in the laundry basket later, doubling his initiation ceremony. Slowly the water crept up the plastic window. It had begun to get serious. Chad was helpless and terrified. Someone hissed,

'Turn it off!'

No one moved. The water kept rising and the initiate's eyes were popping. Suddenly someone leapt forward and went to release the lever to open the door. Instead, he turned the machine on, and the whole barrel began to move in a circular motion. He was screaming soundlessly through the transparent door. Trying to walk along the tumbling barrel, he kept losing his footing and falling over.

Suddenly a shout from the other side of the room broke the spell. It was Bill, the Launderer. He rushed over and knocked the lever off, opening the door. Both water and bedraggled borstal boy tumbled to the floor. Bill caught him. The lad was wet and a bit shaken, he said to everyone, but no harm had been done. Bill did not want this kind of disruption reported on his watch, and he swore everyone to secrecy. The deal was, he wouldn't mention it. The new lad did escape the basket experience, though. Bill wouldn't allow it.

He did not escape another form of torture, though. Because had had escaped the drying-room initiation, it was felt by Lucky that he should undergo another one. This time, it was to be administered in the dormitory, in the evening, every night at 20.00 hours. The new lad had become the House Victim, and was to suffer accordingly. It had been partly to do with his escaping the Basket, but also because of his macho tattoo, that failed to match up to his actual character. The tattoo said, 'I am a hard man', whereas his character demonstrated the opposite. This mismatch had not been lost on Lucky, who saw himself as the House Daddy. He would brook no competition, especially if he could trounce the opposition. He was, like all bullies, a true coward.

Thus, every evening at eight o'clock, Lucky would call the new lad to his bedside. Lucky would be there with his small entourage of acolytes, and he would order Chad to remove his shirt, which Chad would do. He would them command him to turn around. The next order would be to Andy, who would be told to wrap his arms round Chad's sunken chest.

'Now, Chad, take ten deep breaths, holding each one in for as long as you can.'

Obediently, Chad would take the ten deep breaths and hold each one in for as long as possible.

On completion of the breathing ritual, Andy – or whichever one of the circus troupe had been appointed the task that night – would be ordered to squeeze as hard as he could for half a minute.

During these thirty seconds, Chad's body would tremble, palpitate, go limp and collapse to the floor. He would be left in his unconscious state until he recovered and stumbled back to his bed. Some nights, when Lucky had been in the mood, this ritual would be repeated over and over again until his sadism had been satisfied. Whether only once or for multiple times, this would happen every night without fail. One of the repeated ritual's effects was to reaffirm the government of the dormitory by means of fear and threat, but many of those who laughed at the nightly prank were not really laughing, and the mature Roy now wonders if the mature Chad ever took revenge for this abuse, or whether it damaged him so badly that the rest of his life had been wrecked.

He suffered really badly. The whole of his time at Rochester was spent undergoing initiation ceremonies, and some of the indignities he was subjected to were hideous and degrading. He was lucky though. He was eventually discharged in one piece. The House Victim of the neighbouring dormitory was so badly beaten and physically deformed – in the process he was emasculated – that he was released early from his imprisonment. He had been beaten so severely that he was unable to be returned to a communal situation. Whenever the dormitory lost its Victim in this way, Roy, no doubt with others, spent a period of heightened anxiety whilst the next Victim was being selected.

During this time Roy continued visiting the Chaplain's discussion group. He had a good time, and sometimes there would be young women at the meetings, which made it even more enjoyable. It was the first time in his life that he had been a member in a group that shared views and arguments without shouting, fighting or going off with resentment or threats of revenge. No one broke friendships in those meetings, whatever was said. Everyone worked hard at maintaining peace and friendliness.

Listening to those people talking about love and mercy, he once called to mind the House Victims, and learned about the Scapegoat in the Old Testament. This was an animal that the priests put al the community's sins on, and sent it into the wilderness. In this way, the community was cleansed, or forgiven of its wrongdoings. There in the wilderness the Scapegoat died of starvation and thirst, or at the hands of marauders, thieves, bandits or wild animals. The Jesus statue in the chapel, they said, was a carving of God's Scapegoat. He took the sins of the whole world on his back and carried them into the wilderness where he was killed, carrying Roy's, and their, sins with him.

After each of these meetings he would go quietly back to the dormitory and lie in his bed, thinking about things. Why Jesus had to be killed on a cross, as a criminal. The Chaplain had said Jesus wasn't really a criminal; it was just that they trumped up the charge to get rid of him. Roy believed that, though he used to have really heated arguments with him sometimes –

swear at him and tell him he was a liar, or deluded, or mental. But there was no getting away from it; when someone is telling the truth, over time, you know it. The Chaplain was telling the truth.

'Jesus lived a perfect life without any wrongdoing. He was tempted in many ways. Even in those days there were some alluring forces and grim realities in peoples' lives. You think about the various cults and religions that have gone on over time. Then you think about the people who started them or their leaders' lives. All of them fall short. Some of them really badly. That's not only when you measure them against the high standards of God's law, but against their own values and rules. Biographical sketches of these people, some of whom have millions of followers, should only make you wonder how lives so poorly and immorally lived could be so revered by some people.'

He was really letting fly from the pulpit that Sunday. What had inspired him? Whatever it was, it was engaging stuff.

'In contrast to all of them, the life of Jesus stands supreme and impeccable. Some of the greatest scholars in history have recognised this about Jesus. Some of them are Christians, yes, but others are not. W. E. H. Lecky for example, is a non-Christian, but in his book,

'*A History of European Morals from Augustus to Charlemagne II*' he says that the impact of Jesus in unequalled in both what he said and in how he behaved morally. So incredible was this unblemished life that, in an effort to make his own defeated aspirations seem normal, the noted intellectual Nikos Kazantzakis, in his novel, '*The Last Temptation of Christ*', he tried desperately to construct a Christ who succumbed to the impulse of sensuality. Nikos failed in his attempt because he robbed himself of the life changing truth that it was Jesus' purity of mind and life that made it possible for him to provide his empowering grace to humankind. Jesus was not able to save sinners because he was a sinner also. He was able to save them because he was blameless in word and deed!'

Roy, for one, used to leave the chapel after the Sunday service vitalised and renewed. He was beginning to find someone he could believe in. A real man who actually told the truth, and who wasn't afraid to say so.

One night, after one of the discussion groups, he went back to the dormitory and immediately felt that something was different. There was something in the air. It wasn't directed at him, though he didn't know what it was. The idea that it was resentment about him visiting the Chaplain's house did occur to him, but it wasn't that.

Paul greeted him, and they had a play-fight on the floor, as they did most evenings. Then came lights-out, when normally everyone snuggled down and went to sleep, there being no other available light source. Then, one by one, from all parts of the dormitory figures began to form in a circle in the centre of the room. He got up and went to investigate out of curiosity.

About six prisoners had gathered around a huge cigarette. He had never seen a spliff before. He sat down and joined them. The smoke from the large cigarette smelled sweeter than Black Shag. It was pot. Each participant took a deep intake of the smoke and passed the spliff on, holding the smoke deep in their lungs for as long as possible to get the full effect of the drug. Before long the group were out of it. One lad went completely white and was sick. Roy became quite paranoid, and spent the rest of the evening waiting for the guards to drag him to the block and kick him to pieces.

He had no sleep for the whole of that night, waiting for something bad to happen to him. Doors banged and echoed, and voices repeated themselves over and over again in foreign languages that he didn't understand. A firework, which did not belong to him, was launched into the sky, turned into a dragon and ate the moon. It was Roy's fault the moon was missing in the morning. What had he done with it? It was his firework that had done it. Everybody in the street was talking about it, and the police would be coming…

It was work as usual the next day. The episode had passed off with no recriminations. The guards had been completely unaware. However, he would not do that again, thanks very much.

Study

John 1: 13-17. Imagine that you are at that Last Supper table with Jesus, and He comes to wash your feet. What does He say to you? How do you feel? What do you say to Him? Enjoy His attention.

Pray

Pray for new life for all prisoners, especially for young working class, trailer park male and female prisoners caught-up in the web of crime culture. Ask that they may meet with Jesus in these early years of their life.

THE KEY AT LAST

There was still that Chaplain, Hugh Searle. He kept cropping up. Out of all Roy's friends, he felt that he was different. He kept putting him out of his mind, but there he was, right in front again. One day he decided he had better do something about it. Have a showdown. He went to see him.

Putting his cards on the table, he told Roy why he was there in the borstal when he might have had a good job somewhere else. After all, he had a posh Cambridge education and didn't need to be working for the Prison Service amongst convicts. He said his main reason was to help prisoners to find Christ. What did he mean, 'find Christ'?

He said that Jesus was still alive, even though he had died on the cross. He had physically risen from death by God's miraculous power. Roy scanned his face. It was genuine and earnest and true. He could not detect even a trace of the con-man about him. Here was a man who truly and really believed that someone had come alive after dying and been raised from the grave! And he wasn't some ignorant peasant in the backwoods somewhere believing in magic beads, but an intelligent, well-educated modern man who was not at all stupid or gullible.

Was Jesus still around today, then? Yes, he believed he was. Not only that, but he cared about Roy, the person, the individual, the complex creature who made up all that Roy was. Yes, him. Him, himself. Roy the prisoner; Roy the escapee; Roy the victim; Roy the object of scorn and punishment; the Beaten-Up Roy; Roy the Worm; Roy the scum-of-the-earth; Roy the Borstal Boy; Roy the religious inquirer; Roy.

Well, that did it for him.

The Chaplain said that Jesus wanted Roy to become *His* prisoner rather than the prisoner of the Queen. He did not know what to say. This was the big guns coming out.

Roy searched the young priest's earnest face and detected nothing but complete and total honesty and belief. He told Roy that Jesus loved him.

He flushed with embarrassment. He had never been, himself, queer, although he had met plenty who were, especially in prison. But the priest explained that the love of Jesus was not that kind of love. It was a pure and religious love; it was a moral love; it was a pure joy and excitement at being in Roy's company! He could not imagine anyone in the world ever enjoying his company *that* much! After all, he had been a little *shit* all his life. He had no response. Lost for words, he searched the priest's face for even a trace of a lie, but found none. Those eyes were deep and inscrutable honest. He was telling the truth as he knew it, and Roy knew it too.

'Can you accept Jesus as your saviour?' He asked.

Roy looked at his own hands that were torn with labour and hard with calluses from sawing at Reading and working on the farm and in the laundry at Rochester Prison. Did God want these hands, this heart, and my love?

He opened his mouth to say,

'Jesus wants hands like this...?'

But the words would not come. They rose in his throat and gurgled to a stammer. He couldn't voice it. After all these months of putting up a front it had finally come out into the open. He could not pretend any more.

The lump in his throat eased itself into his gut, where it was more manageable. This would be it, then. Spreading his hands on the table, he said,

'Jesus, if you want them, they're yours.'

Then he sobbed quietly. The Chaplain laid his hand firmly on his shoulder and waited for him to finish. There was no hurry. He said a prayer, and Roy wiped away the tears from his face and composed himself for his re-entry into the dormitory among the lads where he would have to pretend that nothing had happened. He would pretend that it was just another discussion group at the Chaplain's house.

Crossing the courtyard in front of the gatehouse he stopped and thought things over. He remembered Reading Detention Centre. How Jesus had been kicked and slapped and spat upon and treated like so much human refuse, fit for nothing but the hill outside the walls of Jerusalem, where they hung Him out to dry. They had kicked Roy in reading Goal. But they had kicked that Man on the cross, even though He was innocent – whipped him with vile and tearing scourges even, until his flesh crawled with his own gore and his guts were torn from his body. He remembered all the nearly three years of lonely nights. He recalled sitting in the corner of the cell after lights out. Sitting there, listening to the screams of the desperate, and the moans and fantasies of the psychiatrically sick, and the taunts of those who had gone beyond despair and entered the realms of the macabre, he remembered his extreme terror. Then there had been the sounds of life beyond the walls; a girl laughing, the sound of the aeroplanes overhead, or the underground speeding by and the hoot, hoot of motor horns, desperately alone. Jesus in the Garden of Gethsemane, where his sweat fell like great drops of blood into the ground as he debated with God about the fate that awaited him in Jerusalem.

Jesus had been lonely and desperate too. He knew what it was like to weep your guts out in the long silence of the night. He was not one who could expect escape or release, for He was already condemned. He had no choice but to suffer and to go on suffering, even when it had become unbearable to him and to those who watched. No-one, not even the poor people who thought that they loved Him, offered a grimy hand. All He could think to say was,

'Father, forgive them, for they do not know what they are doing.'

What a man!

Roy slowed his pace as he approached the dormitory. Jesus Christ, eh? How many time he had used them as swear words. He had never known before what they really meant. He had never known – how could he – that these two words contained everything he would ever need to know about life, love, the truth, and everything in the world. He had not known that this was the Philosophers Stone, the Transforming Moment, the Meaning of Everything, the Ground of Being, and the Meaning of Life. For such a long time he had never known.

Immediately he thought of the millions of others who also did not know. Millions. There must be millions of folk who had been swearing for years about the very Thing that they yearned for – Jesus Christ, the Man who was God. The God who knew what it was to be kicked about, beaten, abandoned, in despair, and alone.

It was at that moment that the phrase, 'Jesus Christ' became a term of love rather than of hate. Roy knew from that moment that he would never use that form of abuse ever again. He just knew.

Study

Luke 23: 26 – 49. This is the most significant event that has ever happened in history. Ask God to give you some new understanding of Jesus' death and its importance.

Pray

For all those lost souls who having searched for the meaning of life, have now found it in Jesus Christ.

HOME LEAVE

In the cold light of day he immediately wished those things had not happened on that Friday night. He wanted to forget it, because it was an embarrassment. He dreaded meeting the Chaplain again. What would they say to each other?

He couldn't forget it, because it had happened, and they both knew it had. He was mostly afraid, not that he had done what he had done, but that he had misjudged the chaplain. Perhaps he hadn't really meant what he had said, but had just had a bad night or something, or had been feeling particularly religious at the time.

If Roy had managed to forget it, his life would have taken a completely different turn. That Friday night proved to have been the turning point in his life and there was, for him at least, no going back. What would the Chaplain say?

At first, Roy did not say anything to anyone. He felt it was better to let things ride and stay cool. It wasn't difficult to do, although there were times when he wanted everyone to know, although he managed to keep it in. Soon his release would come through.

The time came for him to have home leave. He would be allowed to go home for a week to see his family and make contact with the Probation Office in his hometown. From a Home Office point of view, this was a way of setting-up a surveillance plan that would keep tabs on this released borstal boy and that he wouldn't suddenly go missing in the wider community to create havoc wherever he went. Big brother.

For the religiously converted Roy however it was quite a different thing. It was a new start to his new life. He went home and saw his parents for the first time in three years. His home seemed so tiny after all those years. He tried to explain what had happened in his change of heart, but was unable to make them understand. He did not really fully understand it himself, but he hoped they would see something different in him.

His father dismissed it with the comment that religion was a good thing if you happened to be that way inclined. He had been in India during the British Raj, and had seen some stuff. Roy did not know what, but something had hardened him against established religion. Since they never talked together, he never found out what it was. As it was, Roy described his wonderful Friday night experience to his mother, who seemed to empathise if not to fully understand. As far as his father was concerned, he left it alone.

The trouble was, he had banked everything on that fact; that he had discovered the outside edges of something that was true. True religion. If what he had discovered were some awful joke then he would never be able to trust anyone again. When he got to his own family, he discovered that no one except his mother was interested. Even his mother didn't get excited about it. She was kind, but there was no one who really cared what he'd found or whether he had found anything or not.

There he was, suddenly with a hope for the future that he had previously given up as a joke years ago. Now that he had found that hope again, no one he knew was interested. All anyone was concerned about was that he should get a job as soon as possible and make an appointment with his probation officer. Earn some money and satisfy the police. Money! He tramped the streets of Ipswich for a miserable week of Home Leave, looking for work but finding none. His leave came to a close and without a job and with much less hope for the future, exhausted emotionally, he returned to Rochester on the designated train, glad to get back.

He went to the dormitory and lay down on the bed. He conjured up memories of things that had happened on his home leave.

He had walked the five miles to town. He'd gone to the job centre and visited factories looking for work but finding none. No one wanted him, especially with his history. An ex borstal boy was not a safe bet, especially if there was money lying around of an open window to climb through or a car door unlocked. Other people, respectable people, also wanted jobs. Why choose a rebel when you can have someone who had been part of the law-abiding system for years? He had tramped all week looking for jobs and been refused time after time. He did not want to go home, because there was nothing for him there. His only reason for returning would be so the police could keep their surveillance on him. His bedroom at home was no different from his prison cell. Nothing to do and nowhere to go.

He thought of his decision to visit his father. He had a job in a car park. Not knowing which car park his father worked at, Roy had visited each one in town until he eventually found him. It was a crushing experience.

He had only seen him once on his home leave – the day he had returned home. They had not said much to one another. He wandered from his little hut on the car park and gave his son a cigarette. They had tried to talk but the words had not happened. There had been so much to say, but no way of saying it all. Where would they begin? With whose pain should they start? Even more complicated, Roy had wanted to talk about the pain of Jesus, his new Love, and not about his own small suffering. Also, he felt so guilty about the shame and suffering he had brought down on the family. They agreed that the weather was cold for the time of year. Roy said that he should keep himself warm, as he was not getting any younger, and his father had pointed to the single-bar electric fire in his little shed. There was nothing more to say. It was difficult for Roy to believe that this was the man who had written him such profound and understanding letters when he was in prison. He could not fathom what it was that separated them. They had never had an easy relationship. It had always been as though there was a barrier between them. Much as he tried, he felt that he never got close to the man inside his father; the man of tenderness and sensitivity he knew was there. He presented as proud and noble – austere, even. A man oppressed in so many ways by the class he had been born in to, and who had surrendered to a low opinion of his own worth and capabilities.

Roy rubbed his hands together to keep them warm and get the blood circulating. Frozen air billowed from his lips like puffs of smoke and flattened itself against the window before transforming into water-drops. He banged his feet on the floor. His father followed suit. A car arrived and he lifted the barrier. Roy commented that some people had plenty of money too be able to afford cars like that and park them at such prices. They grinned across their separation. His father put a cigarette to his mouth. The smoke wandered up his face, and looking at his watch he said it was dinnertime.

Their eyes met. Father gazed into son and son saw all the longing as clearly as though it had been laid out on the tarmac. He must have seen something younger, less hurt, but similar in the eyes of his son, because a tear came to his eye. He was beginning to grow suddenly old. His hair had turned from rich brown to white in the past two years. His generous moustache was ginger-white and frosted with the cold. They stood together drawing something from one another's hearts and eyes for a moment. He turned his eyes away from those of his child as though he had seen something there that he did not want to see. His prediction of his son's future maybe. He probably saw nothing but destruction and wreckage. It would make sense, considering how it had gone thus far. The son wanted to say,

' I will be all right. I have found Jesus. He will be my guide.'

It pained him that he could not share this with his father. A son who had gone wrong, a prodigal son, though. One who has learned a lesson and returned changed. The time was not yet. The father handed his son a small amount of money and suggested he buy some cigarettes.

Back in Rochester he lay on his bed and wept. He was more confused than sad. How could a person with sensitivity and a brain after a whole life become a car park attendant? Had he been born in to a middle class home, things would have been different. As it was, he joined the army, became a sharpshooter for the British Raj, and became accustomed to having servants. On his return to Britain he was reduced to penury by the Depression and failed to recover. He and his family lived in a slum until a local authority house became available. The ex-soldier never had the opportunity for education, or for the fulfilment of his potential. This would not be so for Roy. For him, it would be different.

But where was Jesus, who would give the key to this new life, to be found. He was not to be found, because it was kept in all the wrong places. His image was paraded at every state occasion, when everyone put his or her best clothes on but no one took His message seriously. He was in the churches and cathedrals, with diamond-studded eyes and Wounds as he hung on gold and silver crosses. He was hidden away out of sight among the middle classes, and behind impenetrable walls of academic achievement. He was safely enclosed in books written for the educated, and preached to the already believing in sermons that only clever people understood. He was in the Grammar and Public Schools, where they had their own special Chaplains - and what was Prison but another part of the Public School system? He was in university lecture rooms, and wheeled out at the start of every Parliamentary Day. He was dusted-off for the occasional wedding, funeral or Christening.

Jesus was an artisan. He was born, probably in a hovel. He lived his life for other people, and died taking the blame for crimes he did not commit. Who was there who cold let ordinary people know about this? Who was there that had such contempt for money that they could work to bring this truth to light?

He lay on his borstal bed and knowing that Jesus was the Key, wanted his class to have it. It looked like an impossible task. Jesus is to the working classes what salt is to a thirsting wanderer. How was it that He had become so far removed from them? Maybe it was because the rich end up with everything and only a few drops trickle down to the poor.

Roy saw something dimly, but it was there, and it was very simple. The deep light that shone out of his father's eyes in the car park that sad day, shone not from the face of a wasted and worthless human scrap-heap, but from the face of Jesus Himself. Jesus, he understood, was present in the very soul of his own father. That light was not the harsh glare of the demand for more money, more goods, and more possessions, however much the working classes deserved, needed or wanted these things. It was the light of a desire for something much deeper, which Roy was beginning to see, reflected in the words of the Bible. The Bible, he had discovered, preached the message that Jesus came to bring good news to the poor and oppressed, to heal sickness, and to initiate people into His special Community. Jesus had not stopped doing that when He was nailed to the cross. Neither did He hang on ornate crosses in wealthy churches with rubies for eyes, diamonds for nail-heads and gold for a cross. He would have been at a loss to know what to do with such things!

His head had been swimming with these things since his evangelical conversion at the Chaplain's house. It was as though he had re-discovered something that his own people had lost centuries ago. He'd dug up a treasure. He'd found a mission, a reason for living. The light of the moon shone in through the bars. There was the wisp of a cloud across the face of the silver disc, and he watched its almost imperceptible precision movement in the still air. After a short wile, he walked over to the window and pressed his face against it, like a child at a candy shop.

He whispered,

'Jesus, if you are alive, and I believe you are, come and heal me. I want to know you. Forgive me for all the things I have done wrong. Give me power, so I can tell by brothers and sisters in every class about you. I know you love everybody however bad they have been. If you are alive, prove it.'

He remained standing at the window for a long time praying. Slowly, he felt, a lot of negative energy and sickness was being drawn from his mind and body. He began to see all men and women as just men and women, and each one a miracle and precious to God. There was no longer any 'working class' and 'middle class'. All were equal. It would be many decades before he came to a deeper Christian understanding of multiculturalism, in which the true worth of distinctive cultures is valued and affirmed. In the meantime, the evangelical imperative was to treat all people in the same way, as Saint Paul had advised Christians, that in Christ there is no difference between Jews and Gentiles, between slaves and free, between men and women. They are all one in union with Jesus Christ. If they belong to Christ, they will receive what God has promised.

From now on, there were no longer rich nations oppressing and exploiting poor nations, but men and women either loving or not loving one another; individuals responding to the urgings of their own God-inspired hearts to needs of others in the world. The world was full of people who wanted the assurance that there was meaning in their existence and that 'Jesus is alive and well.' The call for change in society was no longer the call for a change in the systems by which society was being run, but in the hearts of the individuals within them.

Roy stood at the window and promised Jesus that he would take on the job of letting people know their need of a heart changed by faith in Jesus Christ.

He went happily about his daily work, which now consisted of duties in the Administration Block, situated in the Gate House. There, he managed to get his prison poetry typed by one of the secretaries, who bound it in a folder for him.

Every day he prayed and studied the Bible and read books with Christian themes. His appetite for learning was insatiable.

Spring was coming to a close and summer approached with the promise of warmth and open air, with the freedom to enjoy them. Above all, he had found Jesus. He felt good towards everybody, even the guards. He loved even himself, whom he now knew to have become an honest and truthful person. He felt clean and good. He felt that at last he had come to accept himself, and with that, to make himself even better. He knew that soon Jesus would come again and those beautiful things men and women felt in their hearts about one another would be given the freedom to be expressed without shame or fear of rejection.

He loved Jesus, who had given his empty and meaningless life a fullness and meaning that excelled anything he could have imagined and which overflowed every moment with unutterable joy. It was hard to think that only a few short months ago he had wanted to destroy everything, and had wished that he had never been born.

Now there was nothing like that. He felt he had a fullness of life and a reason for living that would sustain him for the rest of his earthly existence, and would keep him safe for the whole of the pilgrimage that lay ahead. Living water seemed to be bubbling up from within his soul and flow through him, providing such a power of love and mental and physical vitality – of euphoria – that his joy was full to overflowing.

He would offer himself to become a Christian Minister. He would go forward as an Anglican priest to make Christians for Jesus.

Study

John 19: 38-42. Two secret followers of Jesus overcame their fear and took His body for burial. It was a brave thing to do, and opened them to some risk. Are you afraid of someone knowing you're a Christian? However you feel, what is God asking you to do for Him? Sometimes we just have to do it scared!

Pray

Pray for those who are afraid to talk about their faith, or of their friends and work colleagues knowing they are Christians. Remember Christians in prison, and those who have become Christians while serving sentences for crime. Pray for their rehabilitation, ministry, and a positive contribution in future.

THE DREAM – THE REALITY

'Tickets, please.'

The 'please' surprised him as he walked through the railway station exit at the Ipswich terminal and pressed his soggy stub into the attendant's money-stained hand. This was the freedom side of the gate. He felt the train journey had dragged bits of borstal along with it. He had been glad to hear the low hum of the gate closing behind him at the prison. It put a punctuation-stop at the end of the three years, concluding the experience.

His hometown lay before him. Nothing had changed from three years ago, except that it all seemed bigger. The roads seemed wider and the traffic more dense. He remembered how it used to be when he was a child – the slums that ran all the way down to the docks and the River Orwell, stinking when the tide was out and whipping like a snake with deadly underwater currents when it was in. He and his father used to catch elvers and occasionally fully grown eels there.

That was many years ago. Their slum housing had been cleared after the 1952 Spring Floods, destroying what little possessions they had, washed most of the structures away. His family had been given a posh council house some miles out of the now gentrified town centre. Many a day he had spent, skipping off school, playing alone or with a friend on the mud flats at the mouth of the river, not knowing the dangers. All gone. All had been demolished and was past - buried spiritually in his memory, and physically beneath the brand new Fisons Fertiliser Head Office.

At the other end of the bus journey fifteen minutes later, he walked along the street that had been his home. He felt the eyes staring from behind drawn curtains. Or was it his imagination and paranoia? He reached the front gate and walked to the door. It opened before he had time to knock.

He'd had lots of fantasies about that moment. He'd dreamed about it from the start of his sentence. It had always been kisses and open arms. Not from his father, of course. They were not dressed in white, like angels, and they had not bothered to get a cake or to organise any kind of party. What was happening was that one of their children, who had shamed the family and been to prison had come back to the street, and who was to know what new trouble he would be bringing with him? Best to keep it as quiet as possible. Only those who happened to see him coming up the street would know about it. Otherwise, it was best to stay quiet, make sure he got a job and hope he would leave the estate as soon as possible in the next couple of months. Then everyone could get back to normal.

So it was that Roy spent some months out of work, sitting in the tiny front room that was hardly bigger than a cell, staring at the world going by.

The terrible thing was, everyone else was the same. There was a street full of bored and wasting people, not knowing what to do with themselves and lacking the means to find out. The only way to escape from that kind of prison was to be rich, and you don't get rich if you are starting from where they were.

His brothers were at work in the tanning factory. They did not get home until half-past-six, by which time they were worn out. He glanced at the clock. Half past two. Father would not be out of his bed until half past four, when he would want his tea and be miserable. Two hours at least before something happened, and that event would be a miserable one! The dog twitched in her slumber, chasing some imaginary rabbit. The suffocatingly small, dark front room lapsed into a brooding silence. This had been the third week and the sixth day and the fifteenth hour of his new incarceration on a council estate in Ipswich. He couldn't stand it any longer.

'Is that clock right?' He whispered to his mother.

'Ten minutes fast. I keep it ten minutes fast.'

'I'm going for a walk.'

'You want to get yourself a job,' she confided.

Then solicitously,

'You know what he'll be like, with you hanging around all the time, and the neighbours...

'Yeah, yeah. I will soon.'

'Yes, well don't you get into any trouble. If you do, don't bring it home here. We've got enough to worry about.'

He wanted to say he'd changed his ways, but he didn't bother. Why waste his breath?

Out beyond boundary of the corporation estate, walking the dog, he communed with his new Master. Lighting another cigarette, he sat on a five-barred gate and after a long conversation with Jesus became convinced that God had a job for him to do, and that he would need to go and get some education.

'Go and see the local priest and tell him what we've been talking about today, and all about your experiences. Go and see him now.'

The young man immediately took the dog to the priest's house, banged on the door and told him everything.

Returning home later that afternoon, Roy knew that everything had changed. Something had been set in motion that was to shape the rest of his life.

How did he know?

He just knew. The date was July 1966.

On September 22, 1974, he would become a priest in the Church of England at Leyton parish church in London.

Study

Hebrews 13: 20-21. Jesus died and rose again so that you can know Him, love Him and serve Him. He has adventures for you to pursue, whatever age you are. Speak out your thanks to Him today, and tell Him how wonderful He is!

ISBN 978-1-4116-2921-9

9 781411 629219

90000